HAD “THE MOB” MOVED [illegible] FLAXBOROUGH?

Too much violence on the telly? Too many American gangster movies? There has to be some explanation for the goings-on at the Floradora Country Club, some explanation for the rumors of white slave trade and the status game, for the many dirty tricks being played by Town Councillor Crispin and his “lady” on Mr. Hatch and his lawfully wedded wife.

Suddenly an Italian-American with Mafia connections had checked into the Roebuck Hotel. Had he come to town with a shotgun in his suitcase and murder in his mind? Was Flaxborough about to be swept into an orgy of madness and mayhem? The imperturbable Inspector Purbright could divine the letter-perfect truth and trap a killer much closer to home—if only he inspected his mail in time.

MURDER INK.® Mysteries

1 DEATH IN THE MORNING, *Sheila Radley*
3 THE BRANDENBURG HOTEL, *Pauline Glen Winslow*
5 McGARR AND THE SIENESE CONSPIRACY, *Bartholomew Gill*
7 THE RED HOUSE MYSTERY, *A. A. Milne*
9 THE MINUTEMAN MURDERS, *Jane Langton*
11 MY FOE OUTSTRETCH'D BENEATH THE TREE *V. C. Clinton-Baddeley*
13 GUILT EDGED, *W. J. Burley*
15 COPPER GOLD, *Pauline Glen Winslow*
17 MANY DEADLY RETURNS, *Patricia Moyes*
19 McGARR AT THE DUBLIN HORSE SHOW, *Bartholomew Gill*
21 DEATH AND LETTERS, *Elizabeth Daly*
23 ONLY A MATTER OF TIME, *V. C. Clinton-Baddeley*
25 WYCLIFFE AND THE PEA-GREEN BOAT, *W. J. Burley*
27 ANY SHAPE OR FORM, *Elizabeth Daly*
29 COFFIN SCARCELY USED, *Colin Watson*
31 THE CHIEF INSPECTOR'S DAUGHTER, *Sheila Radley*
33 PREMEDICATED MURDER, *Douglas Clark*
35 NO CASE FOR THE POLICE, *V. C. Clinton-Baddeley*
37 JUST WHAT THE DOCTOR ORDERED, *Colin Watson*
39 DANGEROUS DAVIES, *Leslie Thomas*
41 THE GIMMEL FLASK, *Douglas Clark*
43 SERVICE OF ALL THE DEAD, *Colin Dexter*
45 DEATH'S BRIGHT DART, *V. C. Clinton-Baddeley*
47 GOLDEN RAIN, *Douglas Clark*
49 THE MAN WITH A LOAD OF MISCHIEF, *Martha Grimes*
51 DOWN AMONG THE DEAD MEN, *Patricia Moyes*
53 HOPJOY WAS HERE, *Colin Watson*
55 NIGHTWALK, *Elizabeth Daly*
57 SITUATION TRAGEDY, *Simon Brett*
59 CHARITY ENDS AT HOME, *Colin Watson*
61 JOHNNY UNDER GROUND, *Patricia Moyes*
63 THE OLD FOX DECEIV'D, *Martha Grimes*
65 SIX NUNS AND A SHOTGUN, *Colin Watson*

SCENE OF THE CRIME® Mysteries

2 A MEDIUM FOR MURDER, *Mignon Warner*
4 DEATH OF A MYSTERY WRITER, *Robert Barnard*
6 DEATH AFTER BREAKFAST, *Hugh Pentecost*
8 THE POISONED CHOCOLATES CASE, *Anthony Berkeley*
10 A SPRIG OF SEA LAVENDER, *J.R.L. Anderson*
12 WATSON'S CHOICE, *Gladys Mitchell*
14 SPENCE AND THE HOLIDAY MURDERS, *Michael Allen*
16 THE TAROT MURDERS, *Mignon Warner*
18 DEATH ON THE HIGH C's, *Robert Barnard*
20 WINKING AT THE BRIM, *Gladys Mitchell*
22 TRIAL AND ERROR, *Anthony Berkeley*
24 RANDOM KILLER, *Hugh Pentecost*
26 SPENCE AT THE BLUE BAZAAR, *Michael Allen*
28 GENTLY WITH THE INNOCENTS, *Alan Hunter*
30 THE JUDAS PAIR, *Jonathan Gash*
32 DEATH OF A LITERARY WIDOW, *Robert Barnard*
34 THE TWELVE DEATHS OF CHRISTMAS, *Marian Babson*
36 GOLD BY GEMINI, *Jonathan Gash*
38 LANDED GENTLY, *Alan Hunter*
40 MURDER, MURDER LITTLE STAR, *Marian Babson*
42 DEATH IN A COLD CLIMATE, *Robert Barnard*
44 A CHILD'S GARDEN OF DEATH, *Richard Forrest*
46 GENTLY THROUGH THE WOODS, *Alan Hunter*
48 THE GRAIL TREE, *Jonathan Gash*
50 RULING PASSION, *Reginald Hill*
52 DEATH OF A PERFECT MOTHER, *Robert Barnard*
54 A COFFIN FROM THE PAST, *Gwendoline Butler*
56 AND ONE FOR THE DEAD, *Pierre Audemars*
58 DEATH ON THE HEATH, *Alan Hunter*
60 DEATH BY SHEER TORTURE, *Robert Barnard*
62 SLAY ME A SINNER, *Pierre Audemars*
64 A DEATH IN TIME, *Mignon Warner*

A Murder Ink.® Mystery

SIX NUNS AND A SHOTGUN

Colin Watson

A DELL BOOK

Published by
Dell Publishing Co., Inc.
1 Dag Hammarskjold Plaza
New York, New York 10017

This work was first published in Great Britain
by Eyre Methuen Ltd. as *The Naked Nuns.*

Dell ® TM 681510, Dell Publishing Co., Inc.

ISBN: 0-440-17871-1

Printed in the United States of America
First U.S.A. printing—October 1983

SIX NUNS AND A SHOTGUN

Chapter One

The cablegram was addressed to Hatch, Floradora, Flaxborough, England. It read:

> TWO NAKEDNUNS AVAILABLE PHILADELPHIA STOP PERF NINETEEN FIFTEEN STOP EIGHT DAYS OPTION STOP DOLLARS THREETHOUFIVE STOP INSTRUCT LONDON SOONEST STOP INFORMED FOUR NUNS ON OFFER DALLAS STOP WILL INVESTIGATE

The signature was Paice.

Telegraphic communications were so rare nowadays that no one at Flaxborough Post Office could remember whose job it was supposed to be to ride out on the red motor cycle that was propped gathering dust in a corner of the mail van garage. So telegrams, as a general rule, were treated as letters and delivered on the next regular round, with perhaps an extra knock or ring to signify urgency.

Here, though, was a wire that had come all the way from America and, queer as its phrasing was, implied big business dealing of some kind. The Postmaster, appealed to for a decision, ruled that immediate action was warranted, and one of the counter clerks, who lived not far from the Floradora Country Club, was instructed to deliver the cable when he went home for his tea.

Unfortunately, that happened to be a time of day when neither Mr Hatch nor anyone to whom he had deputed authority was on the club premises. The wire was accepted reluctantly by a Miss Ryland, spinster and temporary telephonist of this parish, who said that she would hand it to Mr Hatch's secretary the moment he returned at six o'clock.

Gladys Ryland was one of those people for whom any

unopened telegram is like an over-term pregnancy: they dread learning of something having gone wrong and at the same time fear the fatal consequence of inaction. At the end of twenty minutes' increasingly nervous indecision, she resolved upon a caesarian.

She read the wire through three times very slowly. The only sign she gave of any reaction was a slight shiver. And perhaps the line of her lips had tightened a fraction.

She copied the wording carefully upon a leaf torn from the telephone message pad, folded it twice and put it in her purse. The telegram she restored to its envelope. When Mr Amis, Mr Hatch's secretary, came in at five minutes past six, she handed it to him and said 'I opened it to see if it was anything urgent, but I couldn't make much sense of it, I'm afraid, so I left it for you to deal with.' And Miss Ryland favoured Mr Amis with a smile — of sorts — and he said thank you very much, he expected Mr Hatch would know what it was about, and took the telegram off with him.

On the following morning, Miss Ryland went to the police station and presented her copy of the cable to Detective Inspector Purbright. She assured him — and he said he believed her — that she was not the sort of woman to betray an employer's trust, but she did think that any evidence, however slight, that suggested a white slave traffic ought to be examined and followed up by the authorities.

The inspector, who privately wondered how nuns might be identified as such in the total absence of their habits and what they might be doing in Philadelphia, of all places, in such a condition, promised Miss Ryland that her information would be most carefully borne in mind.

Chapter Two

The Deputy Town Clerk of Flaxborough stared down reflectively upon the satin nightdress case of Mrs Sophie Hatch. Embroidered in black on its pale lemon quilting, her initials — floridly gothic — looked like a request for silence. The Deputy Town Clerk sipped his cocktail, gauged the considerable depth of Mrs Hatch's bedroom carpet by burrowing into it with the point of his shoe, and wondered whether he had been wise, after all, to accept her invitation.

'It usually happens just about now,' said Mrs Hatch. She looked nervously at the clock of the bedside tea-maker, then glanced out of the huge picture window that ran the whole length of one wall.

'Last night, it was exactly at a quarter to eight. Exactly.' She looked again at the clock. It showed three minutes past the quarter.

'Perhaps it's gone wrong. These things often do. It could have gone wrong.'

The speaker was a tall, thin woman in a purple velvet dress that hung upon her angular frame like a dust cover. Mrs Vera Scorpe. Wife of a solicitor. On her face was eager condolence.

Mrs Hatch acknowledged with a quavery little laugh Mrs Scorpe's ingenuousness.

'Gone wrong? Oh, dear, no. It's got a magic eye. That's electronics. They don't go wrong nowadays. Not good ones.'

'Magic eye, for God's sake,' said Mrs Scorpe to herself. She smiled icily at the ceiling.

'Of course, clouds can have an effect,' said a squat, pink-faced man, the branch manager of the bank patronised by Arnold Hatch and his company, Marshside

Developments, and a great pourer of oil upon troubled waters. His wife turned from an examination of the bottles and jars on Mrs Hatch's dressing-table long enough to nod in vigorous agreement.

'Have some more White Ladies,' Mrs Hatch urged suddenly. She grasped the neck of a square, vivid green bottle, and swung it in a general invitation. The Deputy Town Clerk, whose name was Dampier-Small, said 'No — no, really' several times while he held out his glass to be filled. The others made grateful little noises. 'Lovely,' said Mrs Beach, the bank manager's wife, after making sure that her husband was having a second drink.

Only Mrs Scorpe remained aloof. 'White Ladies!' she murmured to her friend, the ceiling. 'I ask you!'

There were eight people in the room. The three who had contributed least to the conversation so far were a Mr and Mrs Maddox and a stout, leathery lady encased for the most part in wool and carrying on her arm a handbag of great size. This was Miss Cadbury, secretary of a local canine charity. She peered into her refilled glass mistrustfully, as if examining a urine sample from a sickly Great Dane. Mr Maddox, manager of the Roebuck Hotel, also looked perplexed but he was enough of a professional to disguise his dubiety as slowly dawning appreciation.

'Do you happen to know,' Mrs Hatch inquired of Mr Dampier-Small, 'if Councillor Crispin and his, ah, his good lady are coming along? I did let them have an invite. That's to say my husband's private secretary did. I think'.

The Deputy Town Clerk was sorry, but he had not seen Councillor Crispin since that morning's sitting of the Highways Committee.

'Never mind,' said Mrs Hatch. 'It's probably her boils again.'

She looked again at the bedside clock. Ten minutes to eight. Mrs Scorpe noticed and smirked.

'Light is a funny thing,' observed Mr Beach, charitably.

'It often deceives the eye.'

'Not a *magic* eye.' Mrs Scorpe was unrelenting in her irony.

'When my husband was manager at the Peterborough Branch,' said Mrs Beach, 'they had a burglar alarm system worked by light. Beams of light, you know. And he worked out a way that thieves might use to get past it. Didn't you, Ted? And they changed the system. Didn't they, Ted? Change it?'

'Well, actually . . .'

'It meant promotion for him, you know. Banks are very security-minded. Well, they have to be. Don't they, Ted?'

Mr Maddox spoke.

'My wife and I have been admiring your, ah, your very tasteful . . .' He gestured vaguely with his glass.

Mrs Hatch's air of anxiety was dispelled momentarily by a smile of gratification. She watched Mrs Maddox gaze in turn at the mother-of-pearl vinyl wall covering, the café-au-lait fitted carpet, the dressing-table in the semblance of a white grand piano (the keys worked little drawers containing cosmetics and the 'score' on the music stand was a mirror etched with notes and clef signs), the midnight blue buttoned-padding ceiling, and, dominating even these wonders, the vast water bed — a round, lung-pink, be-frilled slab that wobbled with the passage of traffic like some incredibly obese ballerina, floor-bound in the final subsidence of the Dying Swan.

'We like things to be nice,' said Mrs Hatch.

She froze, holding up one finger, 'Ah . . .'

The company watched, listened. None moved.

'I thought I heard it starting,' said Mrs Hatch after several uneventful seconds. She was staring at the window. Her face was now decidedly strained.

'False alarm?' suggested Mr Beach, as cheerily as he thought was decent. Mrs Beach shushed him.

From somewhere in the depths of the house there

sounded a peal of bells. It was repeated so quickly that some of the strikes clashed cacophonously. Mrs Hatch stepped quickly across to the window, frowning. 'Oh, I do *wish* they wouldn't press it like that!'

She looked out. A car was double-parked against the others outside the house. It was an exceptionally large car.

Mrs Hatch hastened from window to door. On the way, she gave Mr Dampier-Small a tight smile of satisfaction and murmured to him: 'It's Councillor Crispin; he's here now.'

Somebody below evidently had opened the front door. Mrs Hatch called down from the landing: 'Up here, Harry. Come on, before you miss it.'

'Anybody would think,' remarked Mrs Scorpe in a universally audible aside to Miss Cadbury, 'that she'd got the Queen coming for cocoa.'

Miss Cadbury's expression became even sterner. Flippancy in regard to the Royal Family was reprehensible enough in itself; employing it to belittle a lady whose husband made regular and sizeable contributions to the Kindly Kennel Klan was quite unforgivable.

Councillor Henry Norman Crispin, proprietor of Happyland, Brocklestone-on-Sea, chief shareholder in a north of England juke box company, and substantial owner of two medium-sized hotels on the coast, knew how to make an entrance.

After coming briskly through the doorway, he made a sudden halt, as if unprepared to find so many people in the room, and then stared intently and without haste at each in turn while a smile of mock disapprobation spread slowly over his face. This performance succeeded in conveying the impression of his having surprised them all in the midst of some kind of lewd revel.

Even Mrs Hatch was disconcerted for a moment. 'We've been waiting for it to get dark,' she explained.

Mr Crispin wordlessly signified that this he could well

believe. Mrs Hatch blushed. 'It ought to work at any second now.'

Crispin nodded familiarly at the Deputy Town Clerk and dispensed sly half-winks to Beach, Maddox and Mrs Scorpe. Mrs Scorpe pretended not to like being winked at, but next time she raised her eyes to the ceiling she was looking pleased.

To Miss Cadbury he offered a formal 'Good evening.' She responded with dignity but no warmth. Councillor Crispin she considered, in her own phrase, 'a lustful man'. Had he been handsome also, this would not have mattered so much. Miss Cadbury thought that good looks gave entitlement to a certain boldness of manner; just as warm-bloodedness was understandable in the nobly born. Mr Crispin, alas, was ugly and the son of a Chalmsbury cattle drover. That he had made lots of money did not alter those basic facts so far as she was concerned.

'And what is it,' inquired Mr Crispin of Mrs Hatch, 'that ought to work at any second now?' He picked up one of the heavy cut crystal claret glasses in which the cocktails were being offered and squinted at it indulgently, as if knowing exactly how little it had cost. 'Another of Arnie's little do-it-yourself gadgets?' He chuckled with the aid of some spare phlegm and glanced quickly round the company. 'He's a great boy for public ceremonies, I'll say that for him.'

'Just a few friends that might be interested,' said Mrs Hatch coldly. 'And the installation' — she lingered over the word — 'was carried out by Scuffhams, as a matter of fact.' An arch, absent-minded smile. 'It's a long, long time since Arnold had a tool in his hand. My word, yes . . .'

She realised too late what a hostage she had offered Councillor Crispin's incorrigible vulgarity. He did not say anything. But he had no need to. The grin of comic condolence that turned his protuberant cheeks and chin, bulbous nose and plump jowls into the semblance of a squeezed-up bag of tennis balls was eloquent enough. 'Oh, my God!' breathed the delighted Mrs Scorpe to herself.

Mr Beach felt the sharp prompting of his wife's shoe. He shot back his cuff and stared with exaggerated concern at his watch. 'By jove!' he exclaimed, hoping thereby to discharge responsibility.

His wife leaned towards Mrs Hatch. 'Mr Beach understands electronic installations. Installations in banks tend to be tricky, you know. Perhaps you'd like him to cast an eye?'

Mrs Scorpe noted the immediate flicker of anxiety in the said eye. She hoped that the offer would be accepted. But Mrs Hatch shook her head.

'I'm afraid Scuffhams leave everything sealed up,' she said. 'They'll only allow their own experts to have anything to do with the control system. Well, of course, when equipment costs so much to install . . .'

'Best not to meddle with something one doesn't understand,' Mr Maddox said. Having grown bored with waiting, he was polishing his spectacles upon the clean handkerchief he had taken from his breast pocket. 'What they say about a shoemaker sticking to his last is still true today.'

'Sticking to what?' asked Councillor Crispin.

'His last.'

'His last what?'

Mr Maddox looked flustered. Reddening, he shrugged and gave his glasses another rub.

'Where's Arnie?' Crispin asked Mrs Hatch.

'He's in Newmarket.' The reply was immediate and almost affable. 'Mister Machonochie is running on Friday. In the Pountney Stakes. Pountney — is that right?' She looked about her. 'I can never remember these race names.'

'It should be easy enough to remember the ones that nag of Arnie's has won.' Crispin was grinning into the unresponsive face of Miss Cadbury and trying to offer her a cigar.

Mrs Hatch tilted her head a little and smiled forbearingly into the distance. 'Mr Crispin,' she said quietly and to no one in particular, 'knows all there is to know about horses. So long as they're either going round in a fairground or on plates in the Neptune steak bar.'

The owner of the Neptune Hotel — steak bar and all — suddenly hunched his shoulders and nearly butted Miss Cadbury, who drew back in alarm. Some of his drink spilled on her flank, but then ran in harmless droplets down the resilient wool of her costume. Mr Dampier-Small, instinctively chivalrous, offered her his handkerchief while contriving himself to move to a safer position. Everyone else stared and waited for Mr Crispin, whom they confidently assumed to be helpless in a fit of choler, to launch himself upon his hostess.

Several seconds went by before they realised the truth. Mr Crispin's paroxysm had been occasioned simply by his having laughed in the middle of an inhalation of cigar smoke. Now he fetched a big growling sigh and flapped his hand.

'Christ, woman! You mustn't say things like that!'

He nipped the glowing end of his cigar between a finger and thumb hardened to horn by early years of thrift. He chuckled as he stuffed the butt into a waistcoat pocket.

'Aye, that poor bloody horse,' — he was addressing the company at large, with a special look at Mrs Hatch now and again, as if to invite her expert corroboration — 'that poor bloody horse — what is it you call it again, Sophie? Mister MacWhatsitsname? Anyway, it used to belong to Joe O'Conlon, the bookie. That's right, isn't it Sophie? Yes, but here, wait a minute, do you know why Joe got rid of it? I'll tell you. The poor bloody brute was costing him thirty bob a week in aspirin. That's why. Crippled with arthritis, poor beast. Used to shovel aspirin down its throat through a funnel. Racehorse? Couldn't race itself to the knacker's yard.'

There was a pause. Mrs Hatch patted her tight, blue-grey perm, then stroked the topmost of the three strands of pearls that rode her bosom. Her face, carefully averted from the slanderer of Mister Machonochie, was set in an expression of patient contempt.

'If Mr Crispin has quite finished,' she murmured, 'perhaps you'd care for some more refreshment.' She looked with some puzzlement at the windows. 'I'm sorry our little piece de resistance has decided to be awkward, though.'

Mrs Scorpe echoed the phrase 'piece de resistance' with malicious emphasis upon Mrs Hatch's anglicised pronunciation.

Having shaken the green bottle and found that it was more nearly empty than she had expected, Mrs Hatch stood on tiptoes and looked across heads. 'Has anyone seen Mr Amis?' She caught the blank look on the face of the Deputy Town Clerk. 'My husband's private secretary,' she explained. Mr Dampier-Small shook his head.

'*Secretary*. God help us!' Mrs Scorpe's capacity for sardonic repetition seemed inexhaustible. Hard-mouthed, Mrs Hatch turned upon her.

'Did you say something, Vera?'

'Who, me?' Mrs Scorpe offered a smile like a cut throat. Mrs Hatch looked away hastily.

She went out of the room and to the head of the staircase. She called down.

'Are you there, Edmund?'

A door opened somewhere. She waited until there appeared at the turn of the stairs a slim, fastidious-looking man of about thirty, wearing a formal grey suit. He peered upward. His bearing seemed calculated, like the pose of a photographic model. Two fingers of his left hand rested delicately upon the stair rail.'Did you want me, Mrs Hatch?'

'It looks as if we've exhausted our White Ladies. Would

you mind seeing if there's another bottle? It will either be in Mr Hatch's study or else in the kitchen. Near the bread bin.'

'Very well, Mrs Hatch.'

'Oh, and Edmund . . .'

'Yes, Mrs Hatch?'

She leaned low over the banisters and whispered hoarsely: 'I'm not sure, but I think that you-know-what has gone wrong.'

'No!' Pain and regret were pictured instantly in Amis's face. 'Oh, I *am* sorry.'

He walked out of sight down the hall. She heard cans and bottles being moved about in the kitchen. He returned almost at once and came far enough up the stairs to hand her a second quart of cocktail mixture.

'I do think it's a shame.' He indicated the bedroom door with a nod. 'Especially when you'd asked friends round.'

Mrs Hatch shrugged as she took the bottle. 'Oh, I haven't given up yet. It's a brighter evening than yesterday. That's probably the reason.'

'It *is* brighter. Oh, yes, decidedly.' Amis looked at his wristwatch. 'Which explains why I'm still here. I hadn't noticed the time.'

With a beam of gratitude for his attempt to reassure her, Mrs Hatch turned on the stair and went back to her guests.

By dramatic coincidence, the hush that succeeded her re-entry was pierced by a metallic *ping*.

'Ah!' cried Mrs Hatch. She raised her hand.

The thin whine of an electric motor.

'That's it!' whispered Mrs Hatch. Her face registered something akin to the ecstasy of a rewarded bird-watcher. One finger crooked to direct the company's gaze.

In slow, simultaneous, steady progression across the biggest bedroom window in Partney Avenue moved eight heavy satin brocade curtains, each extending across its appointed area of glass until the last split of pale daylight was obliterated. For a moment or two, everyone stared helplessly into absolute darkness. Then the motor's little song died and there was a second *ping*. Opalescent panels set in the wall behind the bed came to life in a raspberry glow. There was a sudden murmur of admiration.

'It *is* rather pretty, isn't it?' said Mrs Hatch, She, too, was glowing.

Chapter Three

'You were right, love. That creep Hubert was there. Bloody little ponce.'

Councillor Crispin bawled the information back under his left arm. Jacketless and up-sleeved, he was bending low over the pink porcelain sink unit in the kitchen and sluicing water from cupped hands over his red, knobbly face.

In the adjoining dining-room, Mr Crispin's housekeeper smiled as she sorted out fish knives and forks from a big case of presentation cutlery. 'Said so, didn't I?' She breathed upon one of the knives and polished it on her hip.

'Council officials,' said Mr Crispin through the towel, 'ought to know better than go touting around at private parties. They're supposed to be above that sort of bloody thing.'

Mrs Millicent Spain nodded primly as she measured with her eye the spacing of the knife and fork upon one of the table mats before her. The mats were rectangles of cork-based plastic that formed a set of illustrations of scenes from Dickens. The one she had put in Mr Crispin's place showed the Death of Little Nell. His favourite, as she knew, was the Cratchitts' Christmas Dinner, but Mrs Spain was convinced that it was over-fondness for his own wares that had carried off her butcher husband two years before and she had no intention of being deprived of bed and board a second time if she could forestall that eventuality by healthy suggestion.

Mr Crispin came through from the kitchen, tugging down his shirt sleeves. He was grinning at a memory. 'Bugger me, you should have seen old Vera.'

'Vera?'

'Vera Scorpe. She looked like a lady deacon at a farting contest. Christ! If looks could kill.'

He moved behind Mrs Spain on his way across the room and with absent-minded affection squeezed one of her breasts while with his other hand he sorted out whisky from the half dozen bottles on the sideboard. She nudged away his grasp, but not immediately.

'What's for tea, then?'

'Dinner,' corrected Mrs Spain. 'Fish. Well, you can see I've set for fish. A nice piece of baked cod.'

Mr Crispin made his lips look as if he was going to say 'fish' again but he remained silent. He poured quickly a very full glass of whisky, then sat down near the window.

'Let me guess,' said Mrs Spain, 'who else was there.' She pondered a moment, while stroking gently the place lately invested by her employer's hand. 'I know — that awful Cadbury woman from the dogs' home.'

'Right.'

'Yes, well, she's easy. If she doesn't keep to heel she doesn't get Arnie Hatch's subs. What about that fellow from the hotel in East Street, though — nervous man with glasses and a bossy wife — Maddox. I'll bet they turned up.'

Mr Crispin chuckled. 'Aye, they bloody well did. Of course, he's still after the drinks contract at Arnie's club. He's wasting his bloody time, though; I know that for a fact.'

'I wonder,' said Mrs Spain, on her way into the kitchen, 'that those two haven't more pride. Of course, she was a

Hatch herself before she was married. You knew that, didn't you?'

Crispin grunted. He heard the sound of an oven opening and dishes being set down. He sniffed cautiously and with distaste, then thrust his nose into the sanctuary of whisky fumes.

'I remember all the trouble there was over her uncle's will,' called Mrs Spain. 'Amy Maddox was to have got that coin collection of his. They reckoned it was worth over £1000. But it never came to her. It went to Arnie in the end. They never forgave him, Amy and her husband. Yet there they go — sucking up to *her*.'

'Who?' Crispin tried to sound interested.

Mrs Spain's big, gaunt face appeared in the doorway, wreathed in fishy steam from the casserole she carried.

'What do you mean, *who*? *Her*, of course. That awful wife of his. Sophie.' She set down the casserole as grimly as if it contained a human head. 'And don't sit there letting this get cold.'

Crispin obeyed the summons without demur. After a lifetime of what more conventionally domesticated residents of Flaxborough termed his 'arsing around with anything in skirts', he had found a sort of peace in the discipline imposed by the widow of butcher Spain. She was not strait-laced in any moral sense. Indeed, their relationship had begun with a tipsy seduction scene in the upstairs room of "Penny's Pantry" only an hour after meeting each other at the wedding reception of a mutual friend. Millicent adopted much the same attitude to sex as her late husband had shown to meat: one of acceptance, appreciation and businesslike dispatch. Around the house, though, she zealously indulged a love of order, of routine, of propriety, that would have much irked any man already familiar with such matters. Crispin was not. Domestic disorder had always been for him the norm. Now life was crowded with niceties and conceits. Contrary to every expectation of himself and his friends, he found himself actually enjoying them. The transformation had cost him a lot, certainly. But he had made money in the last twenty years like a man shovelling gravel. There was enough to satisfy the social aspirations of ten Millicents. And what, he asked himself in response to her diligent tutelage, was money for if not to secure the benefits of gracious living?

He ate the fish quickly, although it proved more palatable than he had feared. For sweet, Mrs Spain produced an orange-flavoured mousse with whipped cream. Mr Crispin enjoyed it very much. He reflected that Mrs Spain was a treasure, and cast around in his mind for the sort of observation that would please her.

'They reckon,' he said at last, gazing reflectively at his well-licked spoon, 'that old Arnie's trying to sell back that bloody great water bed, or whatever it's called.'

'But they only bought it in March.' Mrs Spain flipped out the information on the instant. 'They had to have special girders fitted. And plumbing.'

'Aye, well, they'll have to have them *un*fitted. Old Arnie's had enough. Every time he and Sophie have some nutty he's bloody sea-sick.'

'Harry! Don't be so disgusting.'

Mr Crispin felt that small warm blow-back that rewards the giver of pleasure. He looked at Millicent's face. It was set in a frown and she was eating with so little movement of muscle that she might merely have been nibbling a stray fish bone. She swallowed and said:

'If you ask me, they haven't done anything of *that* kind for a very long while.'

'How would you know?' Crispin sounded genuinely interested.

'Ah.'

'Go on then, girl. Tell me.'

She unhurriedly gathered together their used dishes. 'It's not a subject I care to discuss.'

He shrugged and turned his chair at right-angles. There

was a leather cigar case on a silkwood coffee table a few feet away. He stretched out a leg and hooked the table towards him. Mrs Spain rose and fetched an enormous ashtray from the end of the sideboard. It was a hollowed out quartz octagon, more than twelve inches across.

'If you must know,' said Mrs Spain, with studied casualness — Crispin smirked at the end of his cigar before suddenly biting it off — 'Mrs Harper who used to do the cleaning at that so-called house of theirs, including the so-called bedroom, told me.'

'Told you what?' asked Crispin, confused less perhaps by the invoking of Mrs Harper than by the implications of "so-called".

'Her son's a policeman. Mrs Harper's son, I mean. And she used to get her meat from us when we had the shop. She reckoned that the Hatches hadn't, well, you know, all the time she'd been working for them.'

'Yes, but bloody hell, they wouldn't have asked *her* to watch, would they?'

'Harry, you're just pretending not to understand. I mean, when people — well, when they behave in a certain way, there are signs left. Usually, anyway. And people can tell when they look afterwards.'

'If they know what to look for.' Crispin drew flame into his cigar without taking his eyes off Mrs Spain's face.

'I think we've said quite enough on the subject.'

Crispin extinguished his match with a great smoke-laden sigh. Gruffly, he cleared his throat. 'Come here, girl.'

Mrs Spain hesitated, then came to stand beside his chair, stiffly upright and with tight mouth. She held in her hands the cloth with which she had been polishing the Scenes from Dickens. In the friendliest manner imaginable, Mr Crispin slipped his left hand beneath her skirt and cupped it round that half of Mrs Spain's bottom which presented itself most conveniently to his attention.

'Mrs Harper,' he told her quietly, 'might have a son who's a copper, but whatever she told you about Arnie and his missus is a load of fanny. Sophie's just the sort of scheming cow who'd keep a clean nightie specially to put out every morning if she thought the hired help was taking any notice. You know what Sophie's after, don't you? The bloody magistrates' bench.'

'A fine so-called magistrate *that* one would make!' exclaimed Mrs Spain, abandoning in the emotion of the moment her attempt to disengage from Crispin's embrace. 'There's more than one in this town remember how she was always having to be brought back from that Polish air force camp out at Strawbridge.'

Reminiscence gleamed redly in the eye of ex-combatant Crispin. 'Remember that tale about the Poles, girl? We were always hearing of women being taken to hospital with their tits chewed off.' He pondered, sighed. 'Now it's Kit-e-Kat and Chinese restaurants.'

'What I can't understand is how she had the face to invite *us* to see her ridiculous curtain gadgets. As if it was the unveiling of a war memorial or something. You should have taken no notice. Gone nowhere near.'

'You got me to ask them round for sherry when we had the portico built.'

'Yes, but not specially to *see* it. That was just coincidence.'

Mr Crispin retrieved the hand from beneath Mrs Spain's skirt in order to scratch his own thigh. He smiled.

'Bloody nearly bust his gut pretending not to notice it was there. Remember? Not that Arnie would know the difference between a portico and a pisspot.'

'There's no call to be crude, Harry. You'll be taken as no better than they are, if you're not careful.'

He pulled a face of mock contrition.

'No, what I can't forgive,' went on Mrs Spain, 'was her looking at the pillars and asking when the builders were going to take the scaffolding poles away. Sarcastic cat. Of course, she'd never got over the way we made them look silly over that so-called swimming pool of theirs.'

'It must have cost him a bloody bomb, having to extend it like that.'

Crispin tugged happily at his nose in recollection. The Hatches, outdone in swimming pool acreage, had been obliged not only to demolish a greenhouse but to sacrifice several feet of tennis court in order to establish parity. What made the affair even more satisfactory was the tendency, shown after only a few weeks, of the older and newer halves of the pool to take part in a sort of continental drift, the result of which was a leakage so considerable that water had to be hosed in continuously at full pressure. Crispin, as member of the General Purposes Committee of Flaxborough Council, was greatly looking forward to hotter weather and its justification of his moving a general hosepipe ban. That would send the bloody tide out, all right.

'Oh, I forgot to tell you . . .'

Mrs Spain went to the sideboard and took a piece of paper from a drawer. 'Somebody from that firm at Chalmsbury rang up today.' She looked at a note she had written. 'Half-past ten in the morning — that's when they're coming to put the Barbecue Barn up.'

Mr Crispin rubbed his hands. 'Oh, marvellous!' He made to reach for the paper she held. 'They know which one, don't they? I don't want a cock-up.'

Mrs Spain peered at the paper, then handed it to him. It was an illustrated brochure. She pointed. 'That one. "The Old Kentucky." '

'Fine.'

'I still think that's prettier, Harry.' Mrs Spain's finger moved to "Ye Olde Trysting Place". 'It says it's got thatch as an optional extra.'

'Thatch my arse. It's not fitted for gas, girl; that's the point. Ours will have a proper barbecue set built in.'

Mrs Spain did not argue the point further. She shrugged, a little sadly, then remembered something else.

'Titch Blossom rang just before you came in,' she said.

'About the car. Something to do with lights.'
'That's right. The Merc. What did he say?'
'He'll pick it up first thing tomorrow.'
'O.K. I'll take the Jag, then.'
Mrs Spain frowned. 'What's he going to do to the lights? They're all right, aren't they?'
'Sure. I'm just having some extra quartz-iodines fitted.'
'And what are they when they're at home?'
'Headlights, my old darling. Just headlights. But extra special ones.' He lunged good-humouredly with open palms. 'Like yours!'
Mrs Spain stepped back hastily, crossing her arms like Joan of Arc. She glanced out of the window at a dark and deserted Arnhem Crescent.
'One of these days, Harry Crispin,' she said, 'you'll do something when people are looking. And then you'll be in trouble.'

Chapter Four

Mister Machonochie was always described in the local paper as "belonging to the Flaxborough stable of Mr Arnold Hatch, the well-known business man and club owner".
The horse had never, in fact, been within thirty miles of Flaxborough. There was neither racing nor hunting land anywhere in the county, whose arable acres were far too profitable to be played with. "Stable", in the context of Mister Machonochie, was merely a courtesy term, a journalistic abstraction. The animal was actually domiciled in a village near Newmarket, where for £20 a week a friendly trainer provided shelter and keep on condition that he was not expected to exercise it in company with his own animals, which he feared might thereby be infected with Mister Machonochie's chronic lethargy (not

arthritis, as Councillor Crispin had slanderously alleged).

This lodging arrangement was doubly convenient. The horse could be entered for an occasional race at the handy Newmarket course, thus maintaining Hatch's status as racehorse owner without placing on the beast the unwarrantable extra strain of being transported around the country. And, as Newmarket was within an hour's car ride from Flaxborough, Hatch could get over often enough to be pictured in the *Citizen* patting the nose of "Flaxborough's hope for the Pountney Stakes" early each May and stroking the neck of the "local fancy for the Bruce Montgomery Handicap" in October.

In this year's Pountney, Mister Machonochie had cantered home an easy eighth. After allowing it to rest near the post and get its breath back, Hatch gave it the large piece of crystallised pineapple procured for the occasion by his wife (whose interest in the turf did not extend to actually stepping on it) and, committing the animal to the care of the friendly trainer for another six months, he made his way to the owners' car park.

Arnold Hatch's car was called a Fairway Executive. It was fitted with a refrigerator, a duplicating machine and a telephone.

Hatch slung into a corner of the back seat his race-going equipment: a light tweed topcoat, binoculars, shooting stick, and the cap that Councillor Crispin called his Ratcatcher's Special. Removal of the cap displayed hair the colour of yellowing linen. It looked the kind of hair that would persist, unthinning, until death. It complemented the healthy pink skin of the face, the calm pale blue eyes, lightly fringed with almost white lashes, and the eyebrows of the same colour that seemed to have been deliberately selected as accessories of taste.

The face, one would have thought, of a man of wealth and discrimination and power; of a merchant banker, say, or a slum landlord of the older, better sort.

The voice did not match.

'Eddie? Is that you, Eddie? This is Mister Hatch talking. I'm at the racecourse as of now . . . aye, the racecourse . . . You what? . . No, he didn't. The going was wrong for him after all that rain. Anyway, what I want you to do is to ring the missus at her sister's and tell her I'll be back in the morning. Another thing. I'd like you to call at the house tomorrow at about ten. I've a special little job for you. Right, then. This is Mister Hatch over and out.'

He hesitated before replacing the phone, as if uncertain of the rightness of the farewell phrase. Then he settled himself upon the genuine calf of the specially built-up driving seat (Hatch was, in Councillor Crispin's lamentable vocabulary, a short-arse) and started the motor.

The hotel at which he always stayed on his excursions in the role of racehorse owner was not, in general, patronised by racing men. Mr Hatch found this satisfactory for two reasons. He was not inconvenienced by seasonal crush. And he was spared the indignity of being associated by the company with an animal that had sense neither of duty nor of occasion.

After an early dinner, he saw and acknowledged in the lounge a man called Baxter. They ordered whiskies and lit cigars. Baxter smoked his with determination and obvious enjoyment. Hatch drew upon his just often enough to maintain its life; the action seemed one of charity, judicious and economical.

The previous evening, Baxter, who claimed to be the director of two companies in the field of food manufacture, had spoken enthusiastically of the benefits that his firms had derived from the advice of a business efficiency consultant. He now expanded the theme.

'These fellows can see the whole thing in a fresh way from the outside. I used to think it was just a gimmick, but it's really marvellous what they can put a finger on profitwise and efficiencywise. They go right through the whole set-up — factories, sales department, social welfare, personnel — top management and all, they don't spare the likes of us, old man. And they beaver on with their little sliderules and work out how much percentagewise the chocolate biscuit production drops when the mix manager's wife has to wait an extra six months for a new coat. Oh, you can smile, old man (Hatch was not, in fact) but it all adds up viabilitywise, it really does. Well, you wouldn't get the really big boys — IBM and Shell and Vesco and so on — doing consultancy budgetising if it didn't pay off.'

Hatch agreed that this was a sensible deduction. Baxter seemed an eminently sensible man, even if he did have a plummy, booming voice that proclaimed, or so Hatch thought, education at a posh school.

'Funny, really, that you should have brought this up,' Hatch said, looking at his cigar to see if it needed any more oxygen just yet, 'because if I recall rightly I've a note on my diary at the office to give instructions on this very subject to my private secretary.'

'You don't say!' Baxter quickly sluiced down his surprise with what remained of his whisky. 'Another?' He indicated Hatch's glass. Hatch drank up. Baxter stretched and peered across the lounge as if it were the Gobi desert. Detecting a waiter, he raised his arm, made snapping noises with fingers.

The waiter stared back with mild interest for half a minute or so, then made leisurely approach. He looked at Baxter's hand.

'I like yer castanets, mate. Wotcher do next — dance on yer soddin' 'at?'

'This gentleman and I,' said Baxter, coldly and carefully, 'would like two whiskies, please. Doubles, if you would be so good.'

When the waiter had ambled away, tractable but unimpressed, Baxter said: 'Fucking peasant.'

'Aye,' said Hatch, glad that Baxter was able so quickly to sound at ease again.

They resumed their conversation. Hatch said that it was his intention to instruct his private secretary to get him the facts about these business efficiency organisations.

Management consultants, actually, Baxter amended.

Yes, well, that might be so, but what Hatch wanted was to know which was the top firm, the best.

'No argument about that,' replied Baxter. 'Mackintosh Brooke. By a mile. It's *the* one. Only question is' — he puffed out shiny, blue-grey, cheeks — 'whether for what you have in mind it isn't, well, too pricey, if you don't mind my talking frankly. MB do come expensive, sure. On the other hand, they're American and they're the best.'

Their fresh drinks arrived. They were brought not by the waiter, but by a girl from the bar in the next room. She was round-faced, plump, and eager to please. After setting down the two glasses, she wiped her hand down one thigh in a long, slow, preening gesture and smiled dewily at both men in turn while she waited for the money.

Baxter leaned far back in his chair, turning a little sideways as he delved into his trousers pocket with his right hand. With the left he grasped his crotch. This burrowing for coin was so laboriously done that sweat shone on Baxter's forehead, now bright red. He stared all the time into the girl's face.

'These what d'you call them, these consultants,' Hatch said, pretending not to notice Baxter's overtures. 'What exactly do they offer?'

'An analysis,' Baxter said. He extricated his hand at last. The coins it held were not enough. With a facility that was almost conjuror-like after the struggle with his trousers, he produced a slim black wallet and slicked from it a note.

'When I say analysis, though,' went on Baxter, looking not at Hatch but at the girl, 'I think what they mean is something pretty elaborate. They talk about a study of management problems.' He waved away the girl's offer to give change. She bobbed her thanks and turned. Both men watched the departure of a prettily undulating rump. 'I'd say we'd be all right there tonight,' said Baxter. He sounded hungry.

'Management problems, you said,' Hatch prompted.

Baxter made a growling sound as the girl disappeared round a partition that separated the lounge from the bar. He gave Hatch attention again with his small, speculative eyes. 'Sorry about that, old man. Where were we? Problems . . .' He took a gulp of whisky.

'Of management.'

'Yeah — sure. Mind you, when these people talk of management, they mean right across the board. Design of products. Profitability. Marketing. Public relations. All that. And personnel. Personnel — hellishly important.'

'But it's only the really big firms that find it worth while to hire these consultants, surely. Isn't what they do some kind of time and motion lark? I mean, they can dress it up, but that's what it is, isn't it.'

Baxter's smile proclaimed a vast worldly knowledge, leavened with tolerance and a desire to help others. 'Look,' he said quietly, 'I don't have to tell you that businesswise everything must either get bigger or just fold up. To get big, you've got to have efficiency. You and I think we know what efficiency is. But we don't. We're too close in.'

Hatch set his lips in a pout of shrewd understanding. At the same time, he noticed both glasses were empty. He pushed the bell button in the wall beside him.

'What *is* your line, if you don't mind my asking,' said Baxter.

'I diversify a good deal,' replied Hatch, using a word that he had heard, liked and stored away a couple of weeks previously.

Baxter nodded emphatically. 'You're bloody wise, old man. Bloody wise.' Then, quite suddenly, his gaze became blank. With his little finger he stroked his thin, black, meticulously trimmed moustache.

The girl from the bar came round the partition. A round tray dangled at the end of her long, carelessly held arm. She put the tray on their table and leaned low to collect the glasses. A white liquidity of breast swung lazily in the dark tent of her dress.

'It would give two lonely travellers great pleasure, dear lady, if you would be so kind as to bring them two-fold potations of the Highland spirit.' Baxter capped this recitation with a grin of grotesque bonhomie.

'Two similar, sir?' She stood upright.

'Whatever you say, dear lady.' Baxter patted the back of the girl's thigh. She turned, but not evasively, so that the withdrawal of Baxter's hand was more like a caress.

When she was nearly but not quite out of hearing, Baxter made his animal growling noise again. Hatch regarded him dubiously but said nothing.

The conversation about business consultants petered out. Baxter was much preoccupied. He drank more whiskies, swallowing them as if conscientiously pursuing a course of therapy. By the fourth round, he had made the delightful discovery that the girl from the bar was quite unprejudiced in the matter of having her bottom fondled.

Hatch saw that his companion would, at any moment now, offer some specious remark about having an early night and trundle away to work his claim.

'Watch it,' said Hatch. His tone, though still friendly, was brusque.

Baxter frowned, grinned, frowned again. 'How d'you mean, old man?' He was swaying very slightly backward and forward in his chair.

'You think she fancies you, don't you?'

'Well, Christ, you could see for yourself. I mean, I'm not going to pass that up, not bloody likely.'

Baxter wiped his palms on his thighs. He gazed towards the bar partition like a lumberjack sizing up his next tree.

'You'll keep clear of that one if you know what's good for you,' said Hatch.

Slyness tilted Baxter's grin. 'Jealous?'

'Don't be daft. I know who she is, that's all. She and her boy friend work the mugs.'

'I like her and I love her little arse,' declared Baxter. Suddenly he scowled. 'Boy friend? What boy friend?'

'He's one of the porters here. Him and Sal run a little arrangement between themselves. Ever heard of Loopy Loo?'

'Sort of nursery rhyme thing, isn't it? Christ, *I* don't know.'

' "Here we come loopy loo. . ." Aye.' Hatch smiled reflectively. 'You'd not like it.'

'What is this, a leg pull or something?' Baxter was showing the petulance of the slightly drunk.

Hatch chuckled, but checked his amusement at once. 'No, no, I'm being absolutely serious. It could be a bit risky to go into details here and now, but what it amounts to is that you'd get cleaned out of money and for damn all. I think it's what they call a heist in America.'

For several seconds, Baxter stared down in silence at the table. He fingered and tugged at a cheek. 'The rotten bloody bitch,' he said quietly, more in wonderment than rancour. Then, after further reflection 'Hell, I'm not going to be imposed upon. I will not be imposed upon. Tell you what. . .' The birth of a splendid idea shone in his eyes. 'We'll share. Take turns. That'll take care of this boy friend or whatever he is.' Cunningly he wagged a finger. 'He won't expect a rearguard.'

Hatch waited for Baxter's giggle to subside. 'Look,' he said, 'if you just want a young lady to tuck in with for the night, you don't have to stay here and get robbed. I can take you somewhere where there's proper arrangements, all nice and comfortable, and a young lady with a bit of tone. As a matter of fact,' — Hatch stood and brushed the lapel of his jacket with his fingertips — 'I wouldn't say no to a nice bit of something on the side myself just this once.'

He began to make his way unhurriedly across the room.

Baxter got up, swayed in puzzlement for a moment, then followed.

He had almost reached the door when the girl Hatch had called Sal came into the room by the bar entrance. Baxter halted, drew breath and crooked his finger as if to summon a recalcitrant infant.

'Hey!' Harsh, angry. Heads turned.

Hatch stood in the doorway, looking back anxiously.

Cautiously and without a smile, the girl approached to within five or six feet. Baxter urged her closer with impatient clawing gestures. She glanced questioningly at Hatch.

Baxter, too, threw Hatch a look, but it was of triumph. To the girl he said, very loudly: 'A word has been said to the wise, dear lady, and the wise has taken heed, so you can sling your little titties elsewhere and play loopy loo all by your little bloody self!' He paused, as if mustering some final crushing indignity, but this proved to be merely a repetition of 'Dear lady,' very sarcastically uttered.

Hatch seized his arm and hastened him out.

'That wasn't very sensible of you.'

Baxter did not argue the point, but he considered his nice new friend was being unnecessarily sensitive.

Chapter Five

Baxter slept deeply all the way to Flaxborough, which they reached just before ten o'clock. Before lapsing into unconsciousness, he had pronounced the Fairway Executive 'absolutely top-hole'. Hatch took this expression of enthusiasm to be further evidence of Baxter's superior — perhaps even aristocratic — upbringing. He beguiled part of the journey with contriving means of showing off the managing director of Sucro-wip Products to Councillor Henry Crispin.

Skirting the broad forecourt of the Floradora, Hatch turned behind the club building and slid the Fairway into his private car port. The forecourt, he had noticed, was closely packed with cars. It nearly always was at this time of night. The club had been a winner from the start.

The original house, a mouldering mansion with fourteen bedrooms and a set of stables just outside the town boundary on Hunting's Lane, had been the hereditary burden of one of the less well-heeled families of landed gentry in those parts until Arnold Hatch, philanthropist, relieved them of it for what he termed 'rubble value' — £300 cash — in 1963. Seven years later, by an interestingly devious manipulation of mortgages, sub-contracts, promissory instruments, share exchanges, hints and threats, he was the owner — at no extra expense whatsoever to himself — of splendidly-appointed premises that fulfilled a never before suspected public need and were the pride and wonder of the town.

He took Baxter on an outside tour of inspection.

'Those lights,' he said. 'We keep them on all night, sometimes all day. Just as well to let people know you're in business. They think the better of you for a bit of display.'

A battery of golden floods gave the front of the building, rich in imitation half-timbering, the appearance of having been doused in maple syrup.

'The missus designed the name-board,' Hatch explained. 'She's mad on flowers. They're a sort of theme of the club, as a matter of fact; you know — a motive.'

Baxter gazed admiringly at Mrs Hatch's creation, the word Floradora across the central façade in letters more than a foot high.

Hatch pointed.

'The first letter — that's made in Forget-me-nots, you see? F for forget-me-nots. Then I think the next one's lavender. Or lupins, perhaps. You can pick them out better in daylight. The R's roses. D for daffodils. She took a lot of trouble over it.'

'Top-hole!' Baxter exclaimed softly.

'The windows on that side,' said Hatch, 'belong to the Wassail Hall. That's an idea that people have taken to in a big way. Medieval banquets. They come from all over for those.'

Baxter, whose inclination to venery had been in no degree diminished by sleep, was beginning to wonder if he had placed too hopeful an interpretation upon Hatch's reference to young ladies. At the moment, it seemed that proprietorial pride was his sole emotion.

'We give them a dagger each to eat their capon with, and a bottle of mulled sack . . .'

'Sack?'

'Aye. Well, it's a sort of modern equivalent. Everybody gets a tankard or a goblet. You see those end windows?'

'Yes.'

'That's where the minstrels' gallery is. I tell you what. . .' Hatch looked at his watch. 'We can go in that way. There'll be no one there just now.'

Only one central light shone in the Wassail Hall. It showed a lofty room capable of seating perhaps 150 people on rough-hewn trestle forms. Set in the wall at the further end was a small railed enclosure, some twelve feet above the ground, the minstrels' gallery. Baxter saw the glint of a drum kit, wires, an amplifier.

Hatch nudged his arm and pointed to a board just below the gallery.

"Gentles, pray hurl ye no bones at ye minstrelles."

Baxter grinned.

There were other notices, all in Gothic script.

"Comforte chamber for ye dames." Another for "ye Esquires."

"Mine Hoste bids welcome to All Goodlie Folk from Ye Tobackow Colonies of Americay!"

'The Yanks love that one,' Hatch said. 'They've a grand sense of fun. One of them told me he'd come all the way from Milwaukee just to see the serving wenches. He said he'd heard back home that they were all descended from Nell Gwynn, but that was just his joke, I expect. On account of the costume.'

'I expect so,' said Baxter. It was with considerable relief that he saw Hatch turn and lead the way to a small door marked "Private: No Varlets allowed".

By means of corridors, they were able to avoid the bars and the gaming section, until they reached a room that seemed to have been designed as a compromise between office and boudoir. It contained a desk of white maple with gilded drawer handles, two small arm chairs covered in floral cotton, a miniature pinewood dresser, a tallboy that could have been (and was) a filing cabinet, a sofa and, whimsically rather than seriously disguised as a Victorian work basket, a safe.

On the dresser tea things were set. A woman sat at the desk. She was softly blowing the surface of the cup of tea held close to her mouth. Her eyes regarded Hatch and Baxter through the steam for several seconds before she put the cup down, revealing a fleshy, high-complexioned face that had collapsed a little through too early adoption of false teeth, but was lively and by no means unattractive.

'Mabs, this is Mr Baxter. He's an executive friend of mine.'

Hatch introduced the woman as Mrs Margaret Shooter, manageress of the club's motel section.

Baxter looked impressed. 'I didn't know there was a motel here, as well.'

Mrs Shooter looked at Hatch, who said: 'Well, there is, and there isn't, if you follow me. We've half a dozen overnight chalets more or less ready for occupation, but we're not officially in business yet.'

'The project isn't finalised,' Baxter translated.

'Aye, that's it, exactly. Anyway, take the weight off your legs, and Mabs'll find us a drink, won't you, girl?'

Mrs Shooter produced whisky, vodka and gin with the air of a perennially youthful aunt, expert in the art of providing audacious treats. She smiled warmly and often upon Mr Baxter, who found himself simpering and shrugging like a callow youth. He liked Mrs Shooter tremendously; she was cuddlesome and sympathetic, and yet stimulatingly cheeky. She moved in a cloud of perfume that made him think of bathwater-borne breasts: white, soapy whales. He did not mind at all her addressing him as 'son'. It was even flattering, in a way. Soon he was calling her 'Mabs' and accepting as perfectly natural her habit of squeezing the inside of his thigh every time she wished to emphasise something or to encourage him to laugh.

Hatch said: 'Bill here wanted to get off to bed tonight with Sally Hoylake.'

Mrs Shooter's amazement wrought an owl-like transformation: her eyes vastly enlarged and her mouth pouted into a beak. 'Oo-hooo-hooo.! Slip-knot Sal.! Hooo . . .!'

Hatch smiled. 'He didn't want to take any notice of me.'

Another hoot from Mrs Shooter. Then she grabbed and held Baxter's knee. 'Good job you did, though, isn't it, son? Christ, yes!'

Baxter hoped that somebody would tell him just what he had escaped from, without his having to ask.

Mrs Shooter, still affectionately grasping his knee, had half turned and was talking to Hatch.

'Funny how young Sal went nasty in that way. Different again from her mother. We were very close, her mum and me. We were in Broad Street in those days.' She burrowed under the lee of her left breast and scratched ruminatively. 'We both worked at the old doctor's place until he got taken off, poor old chap. Now there' — she peered earnestly at Baxter — 'was one of nature's gentlemen. Every blessed inch of him.'

Hatch explained briskly. 'Doctor Hillyard, she's talking about. Dead now — died in prison, actually. Bit of a local scandal.' He frowned and gave a private little shake of the head to warn Baxter that Mrs Shooter might find further reminiscence painful.

'What's loopy loo?' Baxter asked.

Mrs Shooter emerged from sad reflection with another of her high-humoured hoots. 'Hey, didn't you tell him?' she asked Hatch.

'I didn't want him to tangle with Tony.'

She nodded. 'Very wise.' Then she hitched herself forward in her chair and smoothed her capacious lap, in the manner of someone about to tell a bedtime story. Baxter noticed for the first time how white and shapely were her arms, how sensuous her style of moving them.

'Loopy loo,' began Mrs Shooter, 'is a very nasty, mean trick, son, and it just shows how careful you've got to be these days. Now, then, we'll suppose for the sake of argument that I'm Sally Hoylake and that gentleman' — she indicated Hatch — 'is Tony Grapelli, which you'll understand is the name of Sal's business manager. And suppose — just for the sake of argument, of course — that you fancy a nice little gallop, if you follow my meaning, and that you give me the wink that I'm under starter's orders. . .'

She paused, as if to satisfy herself that Baxter grasped the hypothesis, however fantastic.

'Right. So what I do is to go along on the quiet to Mr Hatch here, so that he can make arrangements in good time. He's on the hotel staff, you see, so he has the run of the place and can get into rooms. You follow my meaning?

'When you've had a few more drinks, I slip away with you and off we go to the bedroom where I've led you on to believe that intimacy will take place, but what actually happens is this — and I hope you'll not be embarrassed, because I can't explain properly without being a little bit personal.' She turned. 'Can I, Mr Hatch?'

'Mr Baxter's a man of the world, I think, Mabs.'

'Oh, I *am* glad.' She patted Baxter's thigh in the manner of an affectionate dog fancier. 'I wouldn't like you to be offended, son. Anyway, to cut a long story short, we get into bed in an unclothed state and with the light out and I permit certain liberties that I don't have to describe but you know what I mean, and anyway they're just to encourage you while I reach under the pillow for what Tony — or Mr Hatch, rather — has put there ready.

'The next thing you know, son, is that I've got hold of your little old member of parliament and you think, well, it's only nature and very nice, too, and when you hear me whistle you take it as a compliment.

'But it isn't, son. It's my signal to Mr Hatch down there under the window, which he's left a little bit open. And before you know what's happened, that noose's run tight on your little old m.p. and you're out of bed and being reeled in like a bloody salmon.'

There was silence. Then Baxter muttered 'Christ!' and took a swig of whisky.

'A very nasty trick,' said Mrs Shooter, solemnly. Tucking in her chin, she squinted down at her bosom and brushed away a crumb.

'What would she . . . I mean, what would you do after that?' Baxter inquired.

'Oh, just take my time, son. Put my clothes back on. Go through your pockets and your luggage. Then goodnight and thank you very much and out. There's nothing you'd be able to do. Mr Hatch here would have hauled you tight up against the window, you see, and given his end of the cord a couple of turns round something handy to keep you anchored.'

Baxter paled a little.

Mrs Shooter gave his leg a reassuring slap. 'Mind you,

he'd cast off once he knew I was clear. Mr Hatch would, I mean, because he's a gentleman. I can't speak for Tony, though. Very spiteful, is Tony. He reckons to be a stable lad by trade, but they'll not let him among the horses.'

Another ten minutes passed in pleasant small talk over fresh drinks, Mrs Shooter having switched from tea to gin in order to be sociable. Baxter judged her relationship with Hatch to be professionally correct, yet amiable. He felt sad that Sucro-wip Products had failed to attract managerial material of comparable attractiveness.

'The real reason for our calling,' Hatch said at last, 'is that we're both feeling a bit in need of a sniff at the flowers.'

Mrs Shooter smiled indulgently. Baxter supposed that one of their private jokes was in the air.

'Your Lily's at liberty,' said Mrs Shooter to Hatch. 'And what about Daisy for Mr Baxter?'

Hatch stroked his nose a moment. 'Aye,' he said. 'I think they might do.'

'They're hostessing at the moment, but I can easily take them off. Where would you like to be put? There's seven and eight. Your friend would like number eight; it's lovely and quiet up at that end.'

Mrs Shooter had been consulting a sheet of paper. She now glanced up, as if to remind herself of what Baxter looked like, and added softly to Hatch: 'Unless he's a Special Requirements? Rose is still off with her back, you know.'

'No that's all right. Daisy will do fine.' Hatch gave a friendly nod to Baxter, who was trying not to appear uncomfortable. 'Chef's recommendation,' he said waggishly; then to Mrs Shooter, 'We're not staying, love. We'll run the girls round to my place.'

Mrs Shooter's helpful smile faded. 'Oh, now wait a minute, Mr Hatch. I'm not sure that that's quite on. I mean, this isn't a Chinese restaurant, or something, doing take-away meals.'

Baxter laughed nervously.

'Rubbish, old duck,' said Hatch. He took a pinch of her cheek and wobbled it fondly. She tolerated this intimacy for a moment, then affected impatience and brushed his hand away.

'That's all very well, and I know you're the boss, but I'm responsible for those girls. I like to be sure they're not getting into any trouble.'

'Hell, woman, what do you want — a deposit?'

'It's not wise, Mr Hatch, this off-the-premises stuff. It really isn't wise, I'm warning you.'

Hatch stepped to the door and beckoned Baxter. We'll wait in the car,' he said to Mrs Shooter. 'Send them out straight away, there's a good lass.' He departed in an almost off-hand manner, like a customer pocketing a small and unimportant purchase from a shop. Baxter faltered a few seconds in the doorway, gave Mrs Shooter a little bow and a perplexed smile, and followed.

'You're asking for trouble, son,' said Margaret Shooter to her empty boudoir.

Chapter Six

Mrs Shooter's dire prognostication was fulfilled within the hour in the shape of the most remarkable public exhibition that ever, so far as anyone remembered, had affronted the inhabitants of Partney Avenue and Arnhem Crescent.

The actual witnesses were few, but those few were well able to give pictorial accounts that did justice, and more than justice, to what they had seen. And, as skill in narration increased with practice, the story eventually and joyfully accepted by the town was one of Pompeiian plenitude.

The most significant version, inasmuch as it constituted

an official complaint to authority, was provided by a Miss Hilda Cannon, aged fifty-one, of Lehar House, Oakland, a cul-de-sac off Partney Drive.

Miss Cannon, formerly for many years the female lead of the Flaxborough Operatic Society, was a tall, thin, somewhat desiccated lady, who lived with an ancient mother and five corgi dogs. These dogs she was in the nightly habit of exercising in relays around certain grass-verged roads south and east of Jubilee Park in order that they might, in accordance with their mistress's loyal devotion to old imperial principles, defecate at a safe distance from their own immediate neighbourhood.

She began her third and last trip half an hour or so before midnight. Montgomery, the most malicious of the corgi quintet, had dragged her along the whole of Partney Avenue and some way down Arnhem Crescent before making its first exploratory halt. Miss Cannon adopted the time-honoured stance of dog owners, holding the slackened leash casually at one end while she searched horizons with a cool nobility of visage that proclaimed her utter lack of responsibility for what was going on at the other.

Her gaze happened to be upon the upper storey of the house on Partney Avenue directly opposite its conjunction at right-angles with Arnhem Crescent, when she heard a car draw gradually and quietly to a stop just behind her. The car had come from the direction of Fen Street and the town.

Miss Cannon turned her head just far enough to see the big black shape. The driver had parked on a stretch of the road that was humped over a stream conduit so that the front wheels were higher than the rear. No door opened. The engine continued to tick over softly.

She looked away again, but tightened her grip on Montgomery's leash.

The dog snuffled around in the short grass at the edge of the sidewalk and once or twice squatted experimentally. Miss Cannon resolved to pull it clear and walk on. It was better that Montgomery should be frustrated and even a little vengeful for a while than that she should risk abduction or whatever other unpleasantness the man in the car might be contemplating.

She gave the leash a tug.

At that very second — exactly as if she had pulled a switch — there was a silent explosion of violent white light. The dog jumped and tried frantically to scuttle away.

'Now, Monty! Heel! Stay! Sit!' She sought the magic word. Montgomery bit her leg, but it fortunately was too upset to get good purchase. She managed to slip the leash round a gatepost, then looked about her.

The light was coming from the car's two sets of twin headlamps.

The four fierce beams streamed out along Arnhem Crescent, at the slightly upward angle imparted by the car's tilt, to engulf in sun-like brilliance the upper part of "Primrose Mount", the residence of Mr and Mrs Arnold Hatch.

How very remarkable, mused Miss Cannon. Just like the floodlighting of Buckingham Palace. Was something being advertised, perhaps?

She stood staring up, her thin, severe mouth uncharacteristically slightly agape.

A couple of seconds went by, then all the upstairs curtains of "Primrose Mount" began to move.

In one smooth, synchronous action, they parted and withdrew across the windows. Everything within the room beyond was revealed in bright and sharp detail, like an elevated stage set.

Miss Cannon took a gulp of air as if she had been punched in the stomach. Instinct urged her to shut her eyes, but their lids had been jammed open by shock.

For a while, the four people on stage in the sky above Partney Avenue seemed also to be suffering some kind of paralysis. Frozen in the attitudes in which the searchlights had discovered them, they were not unlike a group of shop window models waiting to be dressed. A more worldly observer than Miss Cannon might have seen a resemblance to a still from a blue movie; one more classically educated, a Greek frieze depicting nymphs and satyrs. She, though, whose imaginative world was no wider than that delineated by musical comedy, was at a loss for analogy: nothing like this had happened even in "The Arcadians".

The two girls in the tableau were the first to recover power of movement. Diane Winge, 16, of Queen's Road, Flaxborough, alias Daisy de Vere, hostess and gogo dancer, abandoned the posture into which she had been cajoled by her new friend Mr Baxter and made what haste she could to get off the water bed. This necessitated a frantic, high-stepping trudge, like that of one escaping from a bog. Never had there been publicly offered such impressive testimony to the truth of Mrs Winge's anxious description of her daughter as 'a well developed girl'.

The skinnier but slightly less agile Lily, who was five years older and correspondingly more practical than Daisy, did not try to rise to her feet but instead rolled to the bed's edge and over it. She thus much reduced the chances of being recognised by outside spectators as Selina Clay, whose father, the headmaster of Flaxborough Grammar School, was a resident of Dorley Road and therefore a fairly near neighbour of Mr Hatch.

Baxter took longest to grasp what had happened and to react to the new circumstances. He first tried shouting 'Put the bloody light out!' over and over again, then, suddenly converted to realisation that the dreadful glare came from outside, he lumbered to the window and began hauling at curtains like a drunken sailor trying to shorten sail.

Two curtains had been dragged from their runway altogether before Hatch was able to persuade Baxter to desist. Then, each seizing and wrapping a ruined curtain around his middle, they retreated hastily to the door and sought refuge in some rearward and unexposed portion of the house.

The girls, tipsily giggling, left their shelter in the lee of the bed and scampered across the floor in pursuit.

About a minute later, the car's lights were dimmed. It drew away as quietly as it had arrived, passed Miss Cannon and made a right turn into Partney Avenue.

' "And leaves the world to darkness, and to me",' she said to herself, feeling by now just a little hysterical. She allowed Montgomery to pull her as far as Fen Street corner. Should she go the few extra yards to the police station and make her complaint there and then? No, better wait until morning, when she would be more likely to find in attendance an officer of rank commensurate with the seriousness of her report.

Miss Cannon began to return the way she had come, urging her dog homeward with a mixture of pleas and blandishments. She was still too far off to notice when the car she had encountered earlier re-entered Arnhem Crescent and drove into its waiting garage.

When she reached the corner of Partney Avenue once more, she looked up at "Primrose Mount". A light moved fitfully about in the bedroom. Someone was using a torch. For an instant, a figure was outlined; the movement of others could be dimly discerned. There was a sudden squeal. Then another. The squeals, thought Miss Cannon, betokened felicity rather than fear. She shuddered.

Detective Inspector Purbright was well aware that there was no need for him to be bothered with reports of mundane misdemeanours. What the desk sergeant had described softly over the telephone as 'a simple case of bishop-flashing, by the sound of it' clearly came into that category. Yet the lady had asked most particularly to see him. It would be discourteous to refuse, so long as she wasn't plumb crazy. And no, the sergeant assured him, she did not seem to be that: she was Miss Cannon, who used to sing for the Operatic. Ah, yes, said Purbright, of course (dear God, that Indian love call!) He'd come down to her.

In the bare little interviewing room next to the cupboard where the constables' wet weather capes were stored, Miss Cannon told her tale.

The light-headedness which had been evidenced the previous night by the eruption in her mind of the line from Gray's Elegy afflicted her no longer. She gave a prosaic, if gaunt-faced, account of the distressing spectacle at "Primrose Mount" and said that she was quite prepared to testify when the police brought the case to court.

Purbright acknowledged at once that Miss Cannon was being very public-spirited in the matter. She would realise, no doubt, that it could be a distressing experience to undergo cross-examination in cases of that kind.

'If,' the inspector added after he had massaged the back of his neck and stared thoughtfully at his finger ends, 'a case does, in this instance, exist.'

'I don't quite see what you mean, inspector. I have told you what I saw. Surely you are not going to suggest that' — she sought the right word — 'that exhibitions of that sort are allowed?'

'*As* exhibitions, no, probably not. But I rather fancy that those responsible were no more eager for you to see what they were doing than you were anxious to be a spectator. Intention, you see — that is important.'

'Someone might not *intend* to commit murder,' observed Miss Cannon coldly, 'but that would be small comfort to the victim.'

'I take your point, Miss Cannon, but the fact remains that homicide and indecency involve differences of definition. You tell me, for instance, that both these men were, as the phrase goes, exposing themselves.'

'They most certainly were!' Miss Cannon's indignant emphasis dashed whatever hope Purbright might have entertained that she was actuated merely by maidenly delusion.

He nodded sagely. 'Yes, well, the law concerning that sort of behaviour contains the words "with intent to insult a female". Two questions arise. One — did you feel insulted, Miss Cannon?'

'Of course I did.'

Purbright raised a hand and tilted his head slightly. 'Are you quite sure? Disgusted, perhaps. But insulted? Think.'

Miss Cannon had a suspicion that the wrong answer could be subject to unseemly interpretation. 'Both,' she said.

'The second question,' said Purbright, 'is this. Did those men *intend* to insult you? Did they even know you were there?'

'Really, I cannot speak for them.'

'Precisely. You do see, don't you, that these matters are not always as simple as they might appear.'

She stared at him. 'If I didn't think I knew you better, Mr Purbright, I should suspect that you are trying to make light of what I saw going on last night.'

'Certainly not. Acts of public indecency are still taken very seriously by the courts.'

'As they ought to be.'

There was a pause. Then Purbright said: 'Policemen are very fond of saying that their job is to enforce the law, not to justify it. You might think that that is too easy a let-out, but I fancy that life for all of us would become much more unpleasant if every policeman were to be issued with a sort of moral truncheon.'

The Mounties in "Rose Marie", Miss Cannon reflected, had never talked like this. She sighed. Purbright saw that his argument had merely perplexed her. He hitched his chair nearer and spoke quietly.

'It was a nasty experience for you. I do understand.

Look — leave it with us now. We'll make some more inquiries. But remember that laws are pretty specific things. They're rather like dog leashes.'

And with this happily conceived simile was Miss Cannon's faith in authority restored. She went out into Fen Street humming "a policeman's lot is not a happy one".

By mid-day, the mysterious irrigation system of Flaxborough gossip was pouring into its main channels descriptions of the Partney Avenue orgy that made Miss Cannon's account sound like an expurgated extract from Louisa May Alcott.

Of the dozen or more girls said to have taken part, eight at least had been confidently identified. Several were fourth and fifth-year pupils at Flaxborough High School and included the daughters of prominent local tradespeople. A lady in Jubilee Park Crescent, nearly a quarter of a mile from "Primrose Mount", was the source of the pungent intelligence that a second batch of girls had been delivered in a car bearing CD plates. Someone else had been vouchsafed a display of nude leapfrog and had heard cries in a foreign tongue, he thought Asiastic, possibly Chinese.

Inspector Purbright, knowing his fellow citizens, inclined to the view that most of the tales were of subjective rather than objective significance.

'Nine-tenths wishful thinking, Sid,' he declared to Detective Sergeant Love, who had been impressed by the volume and sensational nature of the evidence.

Love belonged to that type of cheerful and preternaturally youthful-seeming men who join police forces simply because they want to be with the goodies. In eighteen years' service, his natural guilelessness, like his rubicund complexion, had remained inviolate. Purbright was very fond of him, and supposed that he would have been revered as a holy man had he been born into one of those societies which equate idiocy with sanctity.

'I don't see why people should *wish* things like that to be happening,' said the sergeant. 'Not unless' — he tried out a gay dog grin — 'they're hopeful of being invited up.'

Purbright had not the heart to pass on his finding, based on long observation, that the most diligent discoverer of sin in others was the chronic harbourer of a desire to do likewise.

'What do we know about old Hatch?' he asked instead.

Love considered, then began to catalogue.

'He's a bit of a big noise. He used to be an alderman on the council until they did away with them. Building contracts were what made his money, but they reckon he's doubled it up in the last three years with that club of his on Hunting's Lane. We did him for being drunk in charge in, let me see' — Love gazed aloft and sucked air through pouted lips — 'aye, 1965. They say he's still a Mason, but Bill Malley reckons he was unfrocked, or whatever they do to them, when he was caught fiddling the quantity surveys for that memorial chapel he built for them. He owns a racehorse and a yacht . . .'

'A yacht?' Purbright feared the account was getting out of hand.

'Well, one of those whopping great cruiser things that are moored up beyond Henderson's Mill.'

'Ah.'

'He used to be a Methodist. Nowadays he always wears a sort of banker's hat,' said Love. 'That could be because of his missus, though. They reckon she's mad keen on status.'

'In that case, Mrs Hatch is not going to be very pleased when she hears what her husband has been up to. I take it that nobody suggests she was there last night?'

The sergeant shrugged.

'On the other hand,' Purbright said, 'we mustn't rule out collusion. I understand orgies score quite highly in the status game. Perhaps Mrs Hatch thought it would be nice to have one.'

'Gruesome,' said the sergeant, who had heard the word used a lot the previous evening by a young woman at the Badminton club.

'Go and have a tactful word with Hatch, will you, Sid. See if you can find what actually *did* happen.'

'He'll tell lies.'

'Not a doubt of it. But as long as they are reasonable lies, we can ask no more of him.'

'Shall I try and find out who the girls were? They might be under age.' Love's tone suggested hope rather than misgiving.

'They were probably a couple of totties from his club. You won't get much change there.'

Love went cheerfully to the door. Delicacy of inquiries never bothered him. He had something of the asbestine self-confidence of the Children in the Fiery Furnace.

Before getting on with more important matters, Purbright remained a little longer in private speculation.

Two questions in particula intrigued him.

Whose was the car that had been so fortunately placed as a source of illumination?

And what would happen to him if Hatch — a man Purbright knew to have in his nature that element of vengefulness common to most dedicated makers of money — found out?

Chapter Seven

When Edmund Amis arrived at "Primrose Mount" soon after ten o'clock, he was surprised to find his employer grumpy and preoccupied. Hatch was generally a cheerful, even jocund, day-opener, having discovered many years before that nothing makes people more nervous, and therefore commercially vulnerable, in the morning than somebody else's high spirits. Today, though, he looked as if he had slept late and was determined to get the rest of the day at a cut rate.

'First thing I want you to do,' he said to Amis, 'is to get on to these people by phone and ask them to send someone over. Someone who matters; not a messenger boy.' He handed Amis the card Baxter had given him before a hasty and not altogether happy departure by taxi three hours earlier.

'Mackintosh-Brooke?' Amis sounded as if the name was familiar to him in some discreditable way.

'That's right.'

Hatch regarded him steadily, prepared to quell objection. Amis was a university man — Hatch ("I'll pay for the best") had insisted on that — and he formed opinions by much more complicated and devious processes than did ordinary people. It was nice to own such a clever piece of machinery as Amis. He possessed admirable manners. Partly because of these, and partly by virtue of highly developed business discernment, Amis impressed his employer's friends and intimidated his enemies. So long as Hatch felt on form, which was almost all the time, he allowed himself neither to feel inferior to his secretary nor to show that sense of inferiority by refusing to defer to Amis's judgment. Today, though, he felt shagged. And no bloody jumped-up college boy, with or without a string of letters after his name, was going to tell *him* how he ought to spend his money.

Amis nodded briskly. 'Will do.' Not the least of his natural gifts was a sense of when to keep his views to himself.

For a moment Hatch looked bewildered. Then he scowled and sat down to read his mail, which Amis had brought over from the club.

The room that Mrs Hatch called the study was in fact an office. Conceived by its builder in the 1920s as a billiards room, it was spacious and more plain in design than the rest of the house. The walls were a pale sage green, with gilt sconces set at intervals at head height. A long, leather upholstered settee, originally installed for the benefit of billiards spectators, remained on its platform against one wall. Hatch called it his petitioners' bench. Callers, other than people of obvious importance or known usefulness, were liable to be directed to sit there until Hatch, long delayed by inexpressibly vital affairs, should sweep in and eye them on his way to his desk like a busy vet glancing at the day's quota of charity cases.

When Sergeant Love arrived at half-past ten, he was not disposed of in this way. Secretary Amis invited him to make himself comfortable in the family sitting-room and asked him if he would like a cup of coffee. Love said that he would, thanks very much, and hoped that it would be made with milk, but not with a skin on that stuck to the top lip and then slopped down the chin when you took the cup away.

Hatch, not yet recovered from the alarms and excursions of the night, greeted the sergeant less affably than he normally would have done, but was careful not to appear apprehensive.

'I'm afraid,' said Love, 'that we've received a complaint, sir. Regarding these premises.'

This message he delivered with the brightest air imaginable, as if it were the intimation of a lottery win.

'Really? I'm sorry to hear that, officer. Just what sort of a complaint?'

'A member of the public — a lady, sir' (Hatch nodded gravely: a lady, yes, he'd heard of such people) 'has complained of certain behaviour which she alleges was being committed on your first floor last night. She considers it to have been indecent, as a matter of fact, and I wondered if you'd care to make some observation, sir.'

For a long time, Hatch regarded Love with a mixture of thoughtfulness and mild amusement which the sergeant later acknowledged to be altogether devoid of guilt. Then he grinned openly.

'Whoever this lady is,' he said, 'either she's pulling your leg or else she's one of those unfortunate souls who get delusions about sex.'

'Sex?' countered Love, feeling rather cunning. He had said nothing about sex.

'You used the word indecent, sergeant. Is there some other sort of indecency, then? A non-sexy kind?'

No, said Love, perhaps there wasn't. But the lady wasn't one to have delusions. He could vouch for her being respectable and level-headed.

'In that case,' said Hatch, 'it's clear that she must have made a mistake.'

'There have been other reports, sir.'

'Reports of what? Look here, sergeant, how can I answer your questions if I don't know what you're talking about? Who's supposed to have done what?'

Love would have liked to believe that Hatch's sudden tetchiness was a sign that he was about to crack beneath shrewdly applied pressure. He tried the line that always disconcerted criminals on television:

'Why don't *you* tell *me*, sir?'

'Don't be bloody silly,' said Hatch, and very effectively left it at that.

Amis brought in the coffee. It seemed that he had made it himself. Love peeped over the rim of his cup before Amis handed it to him from the tray. Very milky-looking And not a sign of those wrinkles that warned of a skin that would stick to his upper lip.

'Mmm,' said Love appreciatively when he had stirred in four spoonsful of sugar and taken a sip.

Hatch noticed. 'Good lad, that,' he said, nodding in the direction his secretary had taken. 'He's what I call an instant expert, is Amis. Mention anything you like and he'd be able to write a book about it straight off. I got him from a proper university, you know, not from an advert in the *Citizen*.'

Love drank his coffee rapidly and with evident

enjoyment. Until it was finished he said nothing but looked about him in methodical appraisal of the room's furniture and decorations. The wallpaper, cleverly imitative of tapestry, showed Chinese scenes, with pagodas and junks and dinky little Chinese bridges. There were some oriental-looking things, too, in the big glass-fronted display cabinet on one side of the fireplace: a paper fan, some little ivory coolies, tea cups without handles (or were they slop basins?) and a slinky-eyed gent with a great pot belly.

It was this character — Buddha, Love supposed — that served as a *memento venerei* to bring him back to the subject of his inquiries.

'The complaint, sir — the one I came about — was to the effect that unclothed persons were exposing themselves at one of the windows upstairs. The complainant spoke of two males and two females.'

'Rubbish,' said Hatch.

'You mean there couldn't possibly have been any truth in the story, sir?'

'That is exactly what I mean.'

'And the other reports. They were all wrong as well, were they, sir?'

'Obviously.'

For some moments, the two men looked at each other in silence. Love's expression was a bland compound of politeness, patience and, Hatch thought, utter disbelief.

Suddenly Hatch raised and finger and said 'Ah.' He appeared to be thinking hard about something that had just at that very second occurred to him. 'I wonder.' He smiled wrily.

'Sir?'

'I think I've solved your little mystery, sergeant.'

Love frowned. *His* little mystery? Who said it was *his*, for goodness sake?

'Yes, Mr Baxter did mention this morning before he and his wife left that they'd had a slightly embarrassing moment last night. Nothing serious, but I can see that it could have been the cause of these tales that you've heard.'

'Who's Mr Baxter?'

'Of Sucro-wip. The big confectionery people. He's a director, and quite an old friend of mine. He and his wife were my guests at the race meeting yesterday. They came over here afterwards to stay the night. It was a last minute arrangement as a matter of fact — their car had broken down in Newmarket.

'Now then, what actually happened, as I understand it from what he told me this morning, was this. Oh, and I should explain first that Mrs Hatch was away on an overnight visit so I slept in one of the spare rooms and let the Baxters have the main bedroom. You follow? Good lad. What I'd forgotten unfortunately, was that we'd just had this new Autodrape system installed — you know, it works with photo-electric cells and all that sort of thing — saves you having to draw the curtains and switch the lights on when it gets dark . . .'

Love was so impressed by Hatch's easy acceptance of such marvels of moneyed living that he almost forgave him that 'good lad'.

'Anyway,' Hatch went on, 'it seems that Mrs Baxter felt too warm during the night and instead of doing what you or I would do and altering the air conditioner controls, she got up and tried to open a window. She called Mr Baxter to help her, but all they managed to do was to short-circuit something or other so that the curtains drew back and the lights went on. I suppose that anybody walking about outside would see whatever there was to see. Well that's why such people go out on the prowl, isn't it? In hope of spotting something. They're more to be pitied than blamed, I expect.'

With which charitable sentiment, Hatch rose in intimation that he now had much more important things to do elsewhere.

Love, too, got to his feet, but not so briskly. He scratched his nose with his pencil. 'There were only two people in the bedroom, then, were there, sir?'

'Two,' said Hatch, decidedly.

'Oh.' The sergeant lingered a moment before setting off towards the door. There he turned.

'Do you happen to know,' he asked, 'whether Mr and Mrs Baxter were wearing night clothes?'

A tremor of exasperation was quickly suppressed by Hatch, who stroked his chin and said: 'Ah, a shrewd point, sergeant. I see what you mean.' He considered. 'Obviously, I can't say for certain, but now that you mention it, I shouldn't be surprised if they're the kind of couple who might be a bit unconventional in that way.'

'Like sleeping in the altogether?' prompted Love, emboldened to raciness by Hatch's compliment.

'Aye,' said Hatch. 'As I say, I shouldn't be surprised. Not that I'm being critical, you understand. How people go on when they're married is their own business. I hope we haven't got to the stage in this country where it's a crime not to wear pyjamas.'

Love indicated by a cat grin that he hoped so, too.

'Nice to have met you, sergeant,' Hatch said, as he held open the front door. 'And I'm glad you've been clever enough to clear up this little misunderstanding.'

Back in his office, Hatch found Amis at the tail end of a telephone conversation. He sat behind the big lemon and ebony desk and gloomily watched his secretary.

Amis was a good phone performer. His manner was elegant yet precise. He could, as the occasion required, sound friendly or authoritative, but in neither case did he waste words. The present call, Hatch gathered, was to Mackintosh-Brooke. And it seemed that all Amis's skill in keeping negotiations to the point was having to be deployed.

'That was a wordy gentleman,' Amis commented as he put down the telephone. 'If he's an example of their ideals of business efficiency, they ought to be a sure-fire firm to sick on to your rivals.'

'When are they sending somebody?' Hatch asked brusquely. He looked annoyed.

'Monday. Some characters they describe as Preliminary Prioritizers, for God's sake.'

Hatch's frown deepened. 'Never mind what they call them. You've made the appointment; that's all I want to know at the moment.'

Amis recognised the symptom of danger that his employer's irritation might turn to real anger: the tightening and turning nearly white of a little area round each corner of his mouth and the pulsation there of an irregular tic. He decided to keep to himself for the time being his considered opinion that calling in a firm of efficiency consultants was like inviting household economy hints from a notorious free-loader.

'I'm going over to the estate office at Brocklestone,' Hatch announced. 'I don't know when I'll be back, but there are a couple of things I want you to do. Look up a man called Baxter. He's a director of Sucro-wip and lives in Buckinghamshire somewhere. When you've found his full name and address, send him an account for £25 on a Floradora billhead.'

'Charged for what?'

'Entertainment — just put entertainment. Oh, and send him a Club souvenir ball-point at the same time. That one with the bit of poetry on it.'

Amis fished a pen out of his own pocket and read off: ' "I got Thee flowers to strew Thy way". Right?'

'That's it,' said Hatch. For an instant, he seemed about to smile.

'Anything else?'

'Aye. I want you to make some discreet inquiries at a couple of garages. Try Brindle's and the South Circuit first. Blossom's the bloke to see at the South Circuit. I want to know if anybody has had special high-power lamps fitted to his car in the last few days. And if so, who.'

Amis cocked his head on one side dubiously, as if awaiting explanation.

Hatch shrugged, flapped one hand. 'It's an idea I have, that's all. Nothing important. I'll tell you about it later. When you've found out what I want to know.'

Chapter Eight

On the broad stretch of river held by the lock just above Henderson's Mill, there was taking place what appeared to be some kind of migratory assembly. Men wearing white, high-necked sweaters busied themselves with ropes and mooring pins or groped into engines or lurched along the towpath lugging water canisters and drums of fuel. Their wives, suddenly and, in some cases, astonishingly expanded into the more liberal lineaments of leisure, swilled decks and polished paint. Some of the men wore nautical-looking caps at which they tugged whenever one hand could be spared for the purpose. Cheerful, neighbourly calls echoed along the reach from mooring to mooring and between boats that already were under way and making slow, experimental circles in mid-stream. Their white hulls were twinned by water images bright as new enamel. Freshly laundered pennants hung limply at their staffs, awaiting a breeze to reveal the blue and white and black cipher of the Flaxborough Motor Cruiser Club.

It was a warm, windless Sunday morning in May: the day of the Commodore's Muster.

The Muster was the first event of the Flaxborough boating season. It was meant to be an informal, non-competitive affair that would serve as a limbering-up exercise and a trial of how successfully the boats had survived the winter.

The programme, such as it was, simply required members to take their craft up river one by one in a long spaced procession, to pass through Pennick Lock and continue a couple of miles more to a rendezvous at Borley Cross. There they would pledge the Commodore's health — by tradition at his expense — in the waterside garden of the Ferryman's Arms inn, and return in like order to Flaxborough.

This year's Commodore was Councillor Henry Crispin, owner and master of the cabin cruiser *Lively Lady*. He was accompanied by Mrs Millicent Spain, housekeeper and first mate, in celebration of whose talents below deck (or so Mrs Hatch declared) the boat had been named.

Lively Lady was reputed to have cost £18,000. Its two cabins would accommodate in reasonable comfort a party of eight people. There was a small bathroom, with shower. Television was available. The compact bar had a refrigerated locker. On the underside of the reversible mess table in the after cabin was a film projector. High fidelity stereophonic equipment was installed somewhere, but Crispin had forgotten where the controls were concealed.

There was only one other vessel on the river which was comparable in size, power and appointments. That was Arnold Hatch's *Daffodil*.

This Sunday morning, *Daffodil* had already cast off from the Club landing stage and was cruising very slowly up and down against the opposite shore, her twin diesels throttled so far back that they made no more noise than the blowing of smoke rings in a boardroom.

Hatch sat high in the cockpit amidships, cradled at a relaxed angle in a seat like a dentist's chair. He wore white ducks and a blazer with the Club emblem on its breast pocket. His yachting cap was white as cake icing. On a ledge beside the controls, and within equally easy reach of his hand, was a tall glass of whisky and ginger ale, its outside beady with condensation. Every now and again, Hatch sipped from the glass — gravely, like a priest — while his left hand lingered over a lever or made judicious selection amongst the switches and dials.

A boy in a dinghy ventured carelessly close to *Daffodil's* bow. Hatch touched a button. It produced a bolt of sound so imperious that the boy nearly fell in the river in his haste to pull clear of what he must have supposed an ocean liner.

Mrs Hatch smiled at the boy and wagged a finger in friendly reproof. She was leaning graciously against the rail on the fore deck, from which vantage point she had been making her personal equivalent of a naval review. The results were not without interest.

'You would think, wouldn't you,' she was later to say to her husband, 'that the Maddoxes could have run to something better than that thing he was trying to start this morning.' Mr Dampier-Small had the same little home-made motor boat as last year; no wonder he never brought his family on the river. Dr Bruce was still messing about in an old tub of a converted lifeboat, while Ted Beach — for all he was a bank manager — could only boast a three-berth, outboard motor affair. Most delicous of all, though, was Mrs Hatch's discovery that Vera Scorpe and her lawyer husband were now the possessors — presumably the ignorant possessors — of a boat that once had belonged to the perpetrator of Flaxborough's notorious 'black mass' murder of poor Mr Persimmon, the supermarket manager. She thought she recalled some mention at the time of the trial, of "debts all over the place" and enjoyed for the next few minutes a daydream in which Vera and her husband were forcibly and in public sight dispossessed of the vessel by agents of a hire purchase company.

Her reverie was interrupted by a burst of cheering. Hooters sounded. The owner of a venerable steam launch now bank-bound by age clanged its big brass bell. *Lively Lady* emerged slowly from the cluster of boats at the club's landing stage and slid out into mid stream.

Hatch immediately put *Daffodil* about, bringing her over into the centre channel about three hundred yards in the wake of *Lively Lady*.

Commodore Crispin waved within his elevated wheelhouse in acknowledgment of the club members' salutations. He was smoking a cigar as big as a cucumber. His yachting cap, though quite as clean as Hatch's was much creased and buckled and had a distinctly jaunty, sea-doggy look about it.

'Ahoy there, Joey boy! Tell your missus to get athwart that line or she'll go tit over anchor!'

The commodoreal sally sent a group of ladies aboard bookmaker O'Conlon's launch *Pope Paul* into shrieks of amusement.

'Hard luck on the bloody sharks if *you* fall in, mate!' somebody shouted back. There was renewed laughter. Crispin grinned his delight.

Mrs Millicent Spain, attired in jumper and bell-bottoms and standing by the stern, murmured something that included the word 'common' and frowned steadfastly to starboard.

The stately progress of Crispin's boat put the moorings far enough behind after ten minutes for those on the bank to have become tiny blobs of colour. Then *Lively Lady* passed through the central arch of the bridge at Chipper's Hurn and the two passed from sight altogether.

It was not until they were half way up the next reach that Mrs Spain noticed that *Daffodil* had increased speed and was now only a couple of lengths astern. She shouted to Crispin and nodded back towards the overhauling boat.

Hatch's face was relaxed, slightly bored-looking. He smiled thinly on seeing Crispin turn and stare.

Crispin gave Hatch a friendly wave. At the same time, he eased the throttle lever forward a fraction.

Lively Lady's prow lifted and began to sprout two little wings of spume. The distance between the boats increased. Mrs Spain raised her hand and fluttered three fingers in ladylike farewell.

A few minutes later, she was disconcerted to see that the features of Mrs Hatch, which had been diminished to a small blur by *Daffodil's* falling astern, were once more clear and large. Triumphant, too, reflected Mrs Spain rancorously. She glanced at Crispin, whose face thereupon folded like a bellows into a prodigious wink.

Mrs Spain had to make a quick grab for the rail, so sudden and strong was the boat's surge forward.

Both *Lively Lady* and *Daffodil* had now risen into high-angled racing postures. The twin shouts of their engines could be heard clearly back at the Club stages. Anglers spaced out ahead along the Pennick Level heard them also. A ripple of apprehension passed up their ranks on either shore like an eagre. As the boats approached, the anglers stared at them first with curiosity, then with disapproval, and finally with fury and alarm as they saw their own fate presaged by the abandonment of rods and baskets by comrades downstream in their panic to scramble clear of the great double bow wave that the Crispin-Hatch duel was creating.

Some of the fishermen who had managed to rescue their belongings at first sign of the impending deluge now stood at the bank top hurling colourful obscenities and tightly packed fistfuls of ground bait at the boaters. Several hazarded their lines in efforts to wreak whatever vengeance they could with long casts of hook and sinker. Apart from one luckily aimed ground bait grenade that burst upon and severely discoloured Mrs Hatch's yachting cap, all these attacks were in vain.

Each craft was now being urged at practically full throttle and leaving a wake like a medium warship's. Crispin tried to sustain his lead by zig-zagging from bank to bank, but this manoeuvre lost him just enough speed for *Daffodil*, with a sudden burst of extra power, to slip into a starboard gap and draw alongside.

Crispin's yachting cap had been pummelled altogether out of shape and pulled pugnaciously over one eye. With the other he glared ahead, not sparing the other boat a glance.

Hatch, too, seemed to be indifferent to the fact that the craft were practically hull to hull, but his cap was as straight as ever and he was still reclining in his seat as though *Daffodil* were a carriage in Hyde Park.

The two women, finding themselves only a few feet apart, lacked the excuse of navigational concentration for ignoring each other. Mrs Hatch inclined her head and simpered archly. Mrs Spain responded with a smile as fleet as a camera shutter.

The boats canted on their keels as they roared into a left-hand bend. Then they followed the river right and left again, past a derelict pumping station with a window like a bombed cathedral's, and under a single span railway bridge. In the instant of their passing, the steel girders threw back the sound of the engines as a sudden yell of rage. The women jumped and instinctively ducked their heads.

One more wide bend round a regiment of willows, and the final stretch before Pennick Lock came into view.

It was deserted except for a pair of heron, planing idly over the sedge, and two fishermen, one on each bank, about quarter of a mile ahead.

The towering tail gates of the lock, though nearly as far away again, stood out clearly between water and sky: stark, tarry black, intimidating. The river there looked oily; rags of mist hung about it.

Mrs Hatch did not like locks. For her, they were dark, fearsome chambers of oozing brick, unsafe and God knew how deep, where frail boats were buffeted by a creamy turbulence of water that rose with frightening speed and threatened at any moment to burst back the great timber doors and swill her away like a potato peeling down a sink.

The sight of Pennick Lock, even at a distance of almost half a mile, suddenly turned in her mind what had been a lark into something more like a ride to the abyss.

She cautiously edged her way aft and reached up and tweaked her husband's trouser leg.

'Arnold!'

Hatch gave her a quick, cross glance over his shoulder.

'Arnold, that's enough. Slow down. Let them go.'

He said nothing. But she saw his back give a little shrug of disdain. *Daffodil* did not slow down.

It so happened that Mrs Spain was making similar representations to the master of *Lively Lady*.

'It's not worth it, Harry. They're just trying to provoke you. You're silly to take any notice.'

Crispin leaned out of his wheelhouse on the port side and grinned. In the slipstream, his fat cigar showered sparks like a smokestack. Mrs Spain was put unhappily in mind of a film she once had seen about a mad engine driver. 'Balls!' growled Crispin, fondly.

'No, I'm serious, Harry. Please!'

He jerked back his head and blew clear the butt of his cigar. It sailed in a fiery parabola to hit the water twenty yards behind.

'You pipe down, girl. I'm not giving way to that po-faced git, and he'd better bloody well get used to the idea.'

Hatch held *Daffodil's* course almost exactly in the centre of the river. At the same time, he maintained a speed — not far short of the engine's limit — which kept his wheelhouse a couple of feet ahead of Crispin's. This small advantage was enough to discourage his rival from trying to nudge him further over to the right.

Both women were by now visibly alarmed, but each sedulously avoided catching the other's eye. Mrs Hatch allowed herself instead to be fascinated by the terrifyingly fast approaching portals of Pennick Lock, while Mrs Spain, convinced that her captain had indeed let slip his reason, fumbled with the fastenings of her life jacket and tried to relate sensibly her present peril with things she had read in sea stories about bursting boilers, undertow, and threshing screws.

The calmest figures in the scene were the two solitary fishermen who sat facing each other across the river. They showed none of the dismay that had sent the anglers along Pennick Level clambering to the bank top.

Each took his attention off his line just long enough to give the approaching craft a brief but careful scrutiny.

One nodded. The other made a small acknowledging movement with his hand.

The first angler glanced again at *Daffodil* and *Lively Lady*, then quickly back at the water before him. He reeled in a couple of feet of line.

The second angler paid out a similar length of his line.

Both looked once more quickly downstream. The two boats, roaring nearer, beam to beam, had their prows almost clear of the water. *Lively Lady* was beginning to adopt a lengthwise rearing motion, like an animal at full gallop.

Forty yards to go.

The fisherman on *Lively Lady's* side of the river took measure of the situation with one eye screwed nearly shut. He pulled a little on his line.

Something long and heavy and black that was discernible only at close quarters rolled sluggishly just beneath the surface. It looked like a crocodile.

Twenty yards.

Ten.

Of all the disconcerting things that happened in the next few seconds, perhaps the oddest, if not the most obvious, was a simultaneous action by the two fishermen. Each drew from his pocket a small pair of scissors and calmly, neatly, cut his line.

With a roar and a great flurry of spray, the two boats rushed by.

In that instant, signalled by a sound like a house roof being torn off, their courses dramatically diverged.

Daffodil shot forward on level keel towards Pennick Lock.

Lively Lady rose into the air.

The fishermen gazed admiringly at her levitation, but it was not maintained.

A quarter of the length of her fibreglass bottom ripped open by the crocodile that was not a crocodile but a great baulk of waterlogged timber warty with iron bolt heads, *Lively Lady* flopped back into the water like a gutted fish.

She sank at once.

The river was not very deep along that stretch, and by the time *Lively Lady* had settled stolidly into the slime of its bed the wheelhouse and part of the deck were still above water.

Mrs Spain, who had screamed a good deal and clung desperately to the rail during the boat's last moments of mobility, now appeared possessed of stony calm. Slowly she looked up from the waters that lapped the skylight of the rear cabin. She turned towards the wheelhouse and waited, like a prosecuting counsel confident of the accused's imminent confession and collapse, for Crispin to meet her eye.

Commodore Crispin still held the wheel. Indeed, he was giving it half a turn this way and that every few seconds and muttering to himself. Mrs Spain's righteous wrath gave way to anxiety. She edged her way towards him. The movement made the boat suddenly settle lower into the mud on that side. Water flowed over her shoes. She grabbed a corner of the wheelhouse and pulled herself inside.

She noticed first, and with much chagrin, that a cuckoo clock which she had installed in the forward cabin to make the place look more homely was now floating, cuckoo down, in company with three or four cups and an aerosol tin of fly-killer. She lent closer ear to Crispin's mutterings. They were reassuring. The calamity had not, after all, bereft him of reason, but merely strained his command of language to the point of near-aphasia. She allowed just condemnation its head.

'Well, I hope you're satisfied. That's all. I hope you're satisfied with what you've done.'

'What *I've* done! Good God, woman, are you so bloody thick that you can't see what's happened?'

Crispin's eyes were bullock-like in their indignant protuberance.

Mrs Spain pushed past him and retrieved her cuckoo clock as it was about to float out into the river. She prised open the door above the weed-streaked dial. Its glue softened by immersion, the little wooden bird leered lopsidedly at her for a second, then toppled out and was lost in the flood.

Mrs Spain's pent-up shock and misery found expression at last. She threw the ruined clock at Crispin, whom it missed widely, and wept with long, noisy sobs.

'Oh, Christ!' said Crispin. He abandoned the wheel and put his arm round her shoulders. 'I'll kill the bastard!' he said, apparently by way of comfort. 'I will. I'll kill that sod if it's the last thing I do.'

'Wh-wh-what s-s-sod?' inquired Mrs Spain when emotion had subsided enough to allow articulation.

Crispin grasped her shoulders and held her at arms' length. He peered at her tear-streaked face.

'You didn't honestly think that was an accident, did you?'

'You were going too fast. I told you. I asked you to stop. And now see what's happened.' The floating into view through a partly submerged companionway of a cushion, embroidered with anchor designs, inspired a fresh onset of weeping.

'Oh, shut up, woman. I'll get you another bloody boat.'

She shook her head vigorously. 'I never want to see

this river again.'

'All right. I won't get you another bloody boat. But at least let's get off this one.'

She grabbed his sleeve.

'Harry, you're not to do anything stupid.'

'Hell, what's stupid about getting off a sunken ship, for God's sake?'

'Don't pretend you don't know what I mean. I don't like talk about killing. Not even in fun. Now promise me you'll not do anything you'll be sorry for.'

Crispin made one of his huge hands into a fist and turned it about, examining it with a sort of gleeful exasperation.

'Look,' he said slowly, 'I don't know how he did it, but that bastard set this up for us. It stands out a mile. He's got enough horses in that bloody overblown engine of his to leave us standing. But he stuck right there, alongside. Why? Because he wanted us to be going all out on that particular course, close in. He was crowding us, the sod. And why? Because he knew what was waiting. He'd fixed it. I tell you he'd fixed it.'

'Harry, you don't *know* that.'

'Like hell, I don't.'

'Very well, then. You must tell the police and leave it to them.'

Crispin smiled pityingly at her. He unfurled his fist in order to release a finger to explore his left nostril.

The throb of subdued machinery was in the air. A wavelet moved across the water at their feet and slapped gently against the door of the refrigerated drinks locker.

'Ahoy, there!'

Unmistakeably the voice of Arnold Hatch, thin, dry, a little tinged with embarrassment over the uncustomary Jack Tar lingo, yet tight with secret triumph.

Daffodil, ticking over to hold steady against the gentle down-river current from Pennick weir, was less than ten feet off their starboard beam.

Hatch sat calm as a pharmacist before the controls, and surveyed what remained of *Lively Lady* above water. His wife looked pale and distraught. She kept feeling for stray strands of hair under the peak of her yachting cap, then nervously touching her lips. She shook her head. 'Oh, but its dreadful, dreadful. . .'

'I reckon you've taken some water in there, skipper,' remarked Hatch.

Mrs Spain clutched Crispin's arm. 'No, Harry, don't!' she murmured.

But Crispin was grinning. He shrugged. 'I reckon we have, at that, old mate.'

Mrs Spain glanced at him, then quickly at Hatch and Mrs Hatch and at Crispin once more. Amiability still radiated from the knobbly, knockabout face. It scared her stiff. She heard Mrs Hatch's tearful condolences only as a faint and distant bleat. 'Don't, Harry!' she whispered again.

He chuckled and honked one of her buttocks like an old-time motor horn.

'You're a bit low for towing, I reckon,' said Hatch, after pretence of cogitation.

'We're right on the sodding bottom, mate, that's about the strength of it.' If Crispin had been announcing a prize in a lottery, he could scarcely have sounded more delighted.

'We'd better take you aboard,' said Hatch. 'Chuck them a rope, Sophie.'

'That's very decent of you, Arnie,' Crispin called.

'Least we can do, skipper.'

Crispin gave an elaborate, American movie lootenant style salute. He might have been accepting the surrender of an alien navy.

At her third attempt, Mrs Hatch managed to toss a rope near enough to *Lively Lady* for Mrs Spain to fish its end out of the water with her foot. She handed the rope end, dripping, to Crispin.

She made a final appeal, close to his ear. 'You'll not, will you, Harry? Promise me you'll not.'

He took the rope. His face folded into a smile of reassurance.

'Don't you fret, girl,' he said softly. 'There's more ways than one of skinning a bleeding cat.'

Chapter Nine

It was nearly three weeks before *Lively Lady* could be raised, patched temporarily and then towed down river to Shallop's yard for the greater part of her hull to be replaced. Until then, she was the object of excursions along the bank by inquisitive townspeople and unashamedly delighted anglers.

There was much speculation as to the cause of the accident, which the *Flaxborough Citizen* unequivocally pronounced a 'lamentable occurrence', but the only official authority to show concern was the river board, uncertain of its liability in the event of another boat hitting the wreck.

The police were not notified, nor had anyone thought to associate the foundering of Councillor Crispin's boat with the lodgement, a few days later, of an eight-feet-long timber beam against the sill of the weir near Henderson's Mill. Two boys, hopeful of finding the beam buoyant enough to serve them as a raft, waded out and tried to pull it free, but one of its jagged iron bolts had stuck firmly in a fissure. They splashed back to shore and forgot about the lump of wood and about the two tangles of heavy duty fishing line that were so mysteriously attached to it.

Those who had jettisoned the line felt no regret at its loss, for they were not anglers at all, but gardeners.

One was called Joxy and he was a hard-jawed little

man from Glasgow who, when he spoke, which was seldom, employed a sawn-off-shotgun sort of prose, each statement being propelled by a charge of obscenity. The result was so difficult to interpret that the few people in Flaxborough with whom Joxy thought fit to attempt communication were liable to assume that he was a foreigner and to speak back to him in painstaking pidgin.

The other gardener was a local man, a former agricultural labourer. He was nearly a foot taller than Joxy, with a big barrel chest and broad shoulders, between which was set a disproportionately small head. It looked like a lost ball, lodged in the fork of an oak tree. This man's name was Todd.

Joxy and Todd were employed at the Floradora country club. They were gardeners by definition that satisfied Mrs Hatch's winsomely horticultural logic. Their job was to cull the weeds from amidst the flowers, the weeds being offensive or obstreperous customers. The pair were, in more worldly phraseology, trouble-shooters, chuckers-out, or bouncers.

One day, not long after Joxy's and Todd's expedition to Pennick Reach, there arrived at the club three young men whom the gardeners would unhesitatingly have cropped on the spot had they not received strict orders from their employer to offer the newcomers not merely tolerance but active cooperation.

The three young men were field operators of the Mackintosh-Brooke organisation and they had come to conduct a preliminary feasibility survey of what Hatch had described, in his invitation to the firm, as "our little group of companies".

They arrived at exactly the time that their firm's letter of tentative acceptance had quoted, in an American-made station wagon.

Joxy and Todd, detailed by Amis to garage the thing (they had a curious twin-like propensity for being always jointly at hand whenever the service of either was required), stood together by the club entrance and watched, with sullen hostility, while the MB operators each seized a hard, square document case and athletically disembarked.

Their conversation, such as it was during this brief process, indicated that their names were Julian, Peter and Bernard.

Joxy waited until the new arrivals had marched with springy step into the reception lounge. He jabbed a thumbnail into Todd's belly and the pair lumbered down the steps to the station wagon and opened the door. Inside was a lingering smell of "Camp David" deodorant. Joxy expressed his disgust partly in speech and partly in his manner of crashing into gear and aiming the vehicle for an open door in what once had been a stable for the horses of the Quality.

Julian, Peter and Bernard were being served dry sherry by Pansy, one of the club hostesses, brought in early for the occasion. Pansy did not share Joxy's contempt; she considered that the guests, as she assumed them to be, were as suave, elegantly worldly and well-heeled a trio as ever it had been her privilege to lean low for.

She was not deterred — if, indeed, she even noticed it — by a certain uniformity of grooming, speech and gesture that was displayed by the members of the Mackintosh-Brooke team.

Hatch spotted it at once, this curiously stereotypal quality. It seemed to him that although the clothes they wore were different, one suit from another, they all had been chosen by the same agency or in deference to the same canon of taste. Each man's hair was clean and lustrous as if it had been shampooed an hour before. Handgrips were of equal firmness; all teeth were whole and white; all eyes steady.

Here's reliability, thought Hatch. Here's organisation.

He gave his arm to be pumped by the firm hands. Introductions were brief, yet cordial. Julian . . . Peter . . .

'I'm Bernard.' On billiards-after-dinner terms right from the start.

Hatch glanced about him at the good teeth and dandruff-free hair. He said: 'I've not decided yet, you know, about calling your people in. I just want to know something about it, what you have to offer. That's all.'

Bernard, Julian and Peter looked delighted. Julian took a sip of sherry and gave his sleeve an adjusting tweak.

'What we should attempt,' he said, 'would necessarily be phase-controlled, but first on the board would be a sketch-out of a few basic hypotheses. Naturally, in the final analysis we shall want to zero in on precise issues.'

Peter took over.

'Julian likes to block in the broad-based problem areas,' he explained, 'but let's press a random key here, shall we? It's a big one and it could be a stiff one and the name on it is Personnel. Am I right in suggesting that it rings up some hefty problem-situations, Mr Hatch?'

Hatch tried to look alert. 'Staffing's difficult, certainly. Why, do you have any suggestions?'

'If we were to tell Mr Hatch,' Peter said to Bernard, 'that we have no answers to that one at this present point in time, he would say — and, God, I would be the last to blame him — that we are pretty slow to climb aboard. But . . .' He remained silent, one finger raised, as if he wanted them all to listen to some significant extraneous sound.

Several seconds went by.

Hatch could hear nothing but the chatter of a lawn-mower at the back of the club and the whine of a distant jet plane. He stared at Julian's document case. It looked very expensive.

Suddenly Hatch was aware that Julian had leaned forward and was looking at him earnestly.

'You get Peter's point,' Julian said to him. 'What he's saying is that the input process at this stage of the game is a matter of capabilities. We should take all this right out of your concern area.'

Peter nodded. 'You leave us to worry about exerting leverage impact on the personnel situation, Mr Hatch. It's what we come up with AFTER what we call a targeted dig that will call for your personalised in-slotting.'

'After all,' observed Bernard, 'you don't keep a dog and retain your own bark-function.'

The others grinned in friendly fashion.

'There's one thing I want everybody to get straight,' said Hatch. 'I'm not interested in unloading my responsibility. I like running things. But I don't fool myself that I know it all. We've men in this town — business men, mind — who thought they couldn't learn. And where are they now? Finished. Out. More than one's had a helping kick from me — I make no secret of that. I want to be absolutely frank, gentlemen. I'll pick any man's brains if they're worth picking. And I'll pay the proper picking rate and maybe a bit more. Your firm's supposed to be It with a capital I when it comes to this sort of thing. Right, then. I'll give you a week to have a good look into what I've built up here in Flax. If you can come back to me at the end of that week and prove to my satisfaction that there's a lot more miles to the gallon than I've been able to get — right, it's then that we can start talking chequebook.'

He got up.

'Eddie — that's Mr Amis, my personal secretary — he'll fix up whatever you want. Books, accounts, contracts, stock records — just ask him. He's over at the house at the moment, but he'll be coming back shortly.'

Hatch went to the door and sent Pansy to summon Mrs Shooter.

He introduced her as 'the lady who does all the hostessing arrangements and that sort of thing'.

'We've a motel being built' Hatch explained, 'but the brick delivery position hasn't been too good lately.'

Peter grimaced sympathetically. 'We have to deal with

the up-turn of that particular factor in almost every situation at this time.'

Mrs Shooter watched him as he spoke, then surveyed Julian and Bernard in turn.

'Up-turn is right, son,' murmured Mrs Shooter, not entirely to herself.

'No point in you lads staying at a hotel in town,' Hatch said. 'Some of the motel chalets are finished and properly fitted out. There's a couple you can use while you're here.'

'Very comfy,' Mrs Shooter asserted.

Bernard, Peter and Julian accepted the offer readily. It would, they said, enable their survey to be more productive of grass-roots data. They followed Mrs Shooter through the club lounge – the parlour of the original house, now elongated by an added sun porch that gave a wide view of the garden – and along a covered way to the motel building.

This was a U-shaped block of cabins: uniform, square-faced, concrete constructions. These might have been mistaken for small electricity sub-stations, had it not been for the bright orange or green or purple curtain behind each cabin's single window and the piece of rustic trellis on the left of the door. Only in two cases was there sign of plant life of any kind attempting acclimatisation on the trellis.

The three rows of cabins faced inwards upon a central green, in the manner of alms-houses. A path formed the perimeter of this green.

'They all have a door at the back,' Mrs Shooter said. 'Have to, of course. In case of fire.' She smirked, unexpectedly, at Bernard.

'I thought Mr Hatch said the motel wasn't finished,' Peter said. 'One had expected' – he pouted, seeking the appropriate phrase – 'rather more of a sand and gravel situation.'

'Well, it is and it isn't,' replied Mrs Shooter. 'The idea

at first was to fill in this other side of the square, but what you can see now is finished all right. They're nice. Mr Hatch isn't in a rush to branch out.'

Bernard had produced a board to which was clipped a sheaf of paper. He made a note.

Peter looked back the way they had come. He pondered, half closing one eye, as if measuring something.

Julian said to Mrs Shooter: 'At this present point in time, then, the motel has a non-functional profile?'

'You what?'

'The motel is not being used, in fact?'

'Well, it is and it isn't,' said Mrs Shooter, whose lifetime of trying to please had rendered her somewhat ambivalent as an informant.

'I don't think I lock-in on that one.'

She shrugged plump shoulders. 'You'll have to talk to Mr Amis, son. I just turn down the sheets around here.'

They had halted at the door of chalet number eleven. Mrs Shooter winched up a key from her cleavage and pressed it into Peter's hand. It felt very warm. He nearly dropped it.

She indicated the door with a roguish nod. 'Anyone going to carry me over the threshold?'

The three young men looked blank.

Mrs Shooter knew better than to wait long for pleasantries to root. She reclaimed the key from Peter and opened both the door of number eleven and that of chalet twelve. 'I'll let you have your own keys when you come back to the office,' she told them.

Her re-interment of the master key in its place of safety was effected with considerably less coquetry than had been its production. Nevertheless, it displayed, as did all her actions, a certain stylishness, a quality of flourish.

Bernard made a jotting on his note clip:

Security — sharpen-up master key (motel) situation?

Joxy and Todd appeared, laden with baggage. They

put the cases down outside the door of number eleven and stumped away again. Joxy glanced back from the further side of the square and met the placid but calculating stare of Bernard, note clip at the ready. Bernard gained the impression that Joxy was saying something violently disparaging. He wrote:

Management-staff relations: resentment-eradication?

They examined their quarters. Eleven was larger than twelve and contained two divan beds instead of one. The furnishings otherwise were similar. Each chalet contained a built-in wardrobe, a plain square dressing table and a small bedside table: all new and faced with ivory-tinted plastic laminate. There was a rose-coloured telephone on the table.

Behind a partition of opaque glass, patterned with simulated raindrops, were shower, wash basin and lavatory.

'Adequate,' said Peter, after they had made a rapid survey of both cabins.

The others nodded agreement, then Bernard said: 'You notice the typical provincial negativism in relation to bidet-acceptance.'

'Julian,' said Bernard, 'had better move into the single. He'll need the space on his own for the books.'

'You the accountant, then?' Mrs Shooter asked, making the word sound vaguely spicy.

'Viability assessment,' murmured Julian.

Mrs Shooter regarded him thoughtfully. Her tongue tip grouted around her back teeth in search of breakfast fragments; the effort imparted to her face a disturbingly sardonic expression.

'I could tell you a thing or two,' she said, between cleanings, 'about accountants.' Her gaze shifted for a moment to the one article that seemed out of keeping with the chalet's strictly functional furnishing scheme.

It was a huge, adjustable mirror on a mobile frame

standing close to the wall opposite the bed.

'I suppose,' persisted Mrs Shooter, undeterred by her guests' clear disinclination to be sociable, 'that fellows in dull jobs need a bit more taking out of themselves.'

There was no response. Even Peter, whom she had correctly adjudged sensitive to warm keys, was now fathoms deep in his vocation. He was doing some rapid mental re-reading of the introductory chapter of the Mackintosh-Brooke manual of personnel procedure, "You and the MB Method," for this was his first excursion from the office on a team assignment and he thought he had detected already in his colleagues' otherwise friendly manner towards him just a trace of carnivorous conjecture.

Chapter Ten

'Where — or what — is Flaxburrow, for God's sake?'

'Flax what?'

'Burrow. Flaxburrow. Or borrow. Could be Flaxborrow. Flaxborrow, England.'

'I never heard of it.'

'Yesterday, you hadn't heard of Hamburg, Germany.'

'O.K., so today it's this Flaxborrow's turn. I just shift my ignorance around a little. Keeps it at full stretch.'

Lieutenant Varney and Sergeant Bast would not normally have been conversing in this manner, but for nearly a week they had been closeted together in a mind-punishing exercise known in the police department as nut mail duty. This consisted of making a first reading of all those letters and cards of mysterious authorship and often unintelligible purpose that senior officers, for whose eyes are reserved only the least whacky winnowings, are pleased to call "communications from members of the public".

'This one,' said Bast, after reading and re-reading the single sheet of rough grey paper several times in silence, 'claims to be a tip-off.'

Without looking up from his own pile of messages, Varney waved a tired hand towards one of four wire baskets that lay between them in the centre of the big, battered, burn-pocked table. In this basket already reposed the confident, if somewhat imprecise, announcements of eight forthcoming bank robberies, an assortment of projected homicides, and one kidnapping.

Bast shook his head and gave a little growl of doubt.

'Those are all home territory. This has foreign connections. Maybe West ought to see it.'

Varney looked pained.

'Here.' He reached over, took the paper and leaned far back in his tilted chair, holding the letter close to his belly. As he read, he kept the tip of his nose pressed flat with his left forefinger. Like an elevator button, thought Bast.

'Put it with Assassinations,' said Varney at last. 'That one.' He pointed to the third basket.

A head shake and a negative grunt.

'Why not? Look, Mike, it's nearly five o'clock.'

'Assassinations,' said Bast, 'are for secretaries of state and on up. Ambassadors, maybe. This Flaxborrow — I doubt if it even rates consuls. West would know.'

'And West would keep us here until this time Tuesday. No, thanks.' Varney slid the letter back across the table.

Bast painfully and protestingly hauled himself out of his chair. He clipped the letter to its envelope. With a final look of reproof at Varney, he opened the door and went out.

Captain Jacklin West was accounted the Precinct's oracle whenever matters of political or international nicety needed to be settled. He had been to law school and was, compared with most of his colleagues, a widely travelled man, having once trailed around Europe for a year as one of a diplomat's bodyguards.

Perhaps the long and uncongenial hours spent lurking in solitude outside hotel bedrooms in that era were to blame for Captain West's sole vice: a tendency to prolong conversation. Bast wouldn't know and didn't care. He was rockily conscientious but impatient with overspill ("So damn *rude*, that man," West pronounced him, not without admiration.)

West read the letter and glanced at its envelope. Then he read the letter again, this time out loud, and slowly.

' "Some friends of mine think you ought to know about a certain contract because it is in England in a place called Flaxborrow and these friends think it is wrong and bad for our image if American boys make hits in other countries never mind what the contract has done even if he is a crosser. They think it is a wheel this contract, a British wheel of course, but no name. Also they do not know for sure who is making the hit. I am not a nut this is straight." '

After consideration, West said:

'This letter' (he turned it about in his hand) 'is hand-printed out on a poor quality paper of a kind that might be used in merchandising. Its origin would be hellishly difficult to trace. So would the ballpoint that was used. What you are really asking, though, sergeant, is whether I think it is genuine. Am I right? Genuine, that is, in the sense of being a piece of information on which we ought to act. Right? A piece of bona fide information, in other words.'

'Right.'

'In that case, let us prepare a balance sheet of probability. Don't you think that is the most sensible course, sergeant?'

'I go off duty at five, sir.'

'A logical approach is always the quickest in the end. And let me prove that by telling you that I have already reached a decision by just that process.'

Bast tried to look impressed and was saddened to find how tired he felt.

West took off his square, gold-rimmed glasses and with the tip of his little finger flicked from one lens a flake of dandruff.

'This letter, friend, is not only melodramatic. It is packed with the sort of slightly out-of-date gangsterisms that anybody could pick up from a Mafia thriller. Note the patriotic ketchup. The writer is unquestionably a criminal. I pronounce it a genuine tip-off.'

'So I can leave it with you.' Bast had half turned towards the door. He was scowling. At this end of the day, West's humorous portentousness gave him a pain.

'Sure. I'll have headquarters notify the British police.'

Against his better judgment, Bast hesitated. 'This Flaxborrow . . .'

'Borough,' West corrected. He was scrutinising the envelope. 'Flaxborough. Like Scottsboro.' Then he said: 'Hey, this is the first one of these I've seen. Isn't it hideous?'

Bast looked. Hideous? He formed the unfamiliar word mutely upon an inward breath and tried to fit it to what West was indicating. But how in hell could a stamp be hideous? A little scrap of paper. Who cared, anyway? Or did West mean he considered the representation of the President hideous?

'Saw one yesterday,' Bast said. 'Maybe it's not much like him, at that.'

'I am talking,' said West patiently, 'about the design of the stamp as a whole. Commemorative issues are supposed to have dignity. They are historical documents. That' – he pointed again at the purple-hued picture of the President with Capitol Hill in the background – 'looks more like a for-sale sticker.'

But Bast had noticed something else. He pointed to the hand-printed address. 'He's a joker, this guy. "The Occupier". That's us. And just "Nearest Precinct House".

I've never heard of cops being called occupiers before.'

'Nicer than some of the names we get.'

The sergeant gave a short, humourless laugh and again started to leave, but West's voice beat him to the door.

'You were going to ask me what I know about this little English town.'

'English town?'

'Flaxborough.'

'Hell, no. I just wondered what's so special about it that we suddenly start exporting killers there.'

'I stayed there once.'

'No!' Bast searched the mild eyes behind the big square lenses but they showed only dreamy benevolence.

'The ambassador went up there to unveil a memorial at what had been a U.S. Air Force base outside the town,' West said. 'We stayed the night as guests of the Lord Mayor. Or maybe he's just a mayor, I forget. We fed damn well, that I do remember. The Lord Mayor was in the meat business. A little town with the oldest jumble of housetops you ever saw and a pub and a church every twenty yards, and girls like flowers and very, very slow-moving old men with brick-coloured faces who looked as if they'd have to be hit by lightning before they'd die. And everywhere bloody bicycles.'

He paused, lost in contemplation of bicycling girls, buoyant-breasted in the thin summer dresses of 1958.

'They were nice people.' He shook his head, as if surprised at himself, and reached for the phone. 'Get me Rawlings, of Interpol.'

'Let's hope one of those nice people don't get knocked off,' said Bast, leaving. 'The species is nearly extinct.'

Chapter Eleven

Captain West, of New York City, was not the only policeman to be ready to speak well of the citizens of Flaxborough (England). Their own chief constable, Mr Harcourt Chubb, would have echoed his sentiments even to the choice of adjective, for 'nice' was a word that he used rather in the manner of a talisman, a device to ward off trouble.

'Nice dog,' Mr Chubb would say to any dog he happened to pat. It was really a plea not to be bitten.

On entering an untried restaurant, he would remark to his wife: 'Looks a nice place, dear,' this being his way of trying to beat the fearsome odds stacked against them by the catering trade.

The same abiding sanguinity, or, as it might be said, discounting of experience, sustained the chief constable in referring to the Flaxbrovians in general as 'a nice lot' or even 'a perfectly nice bunch'. If the truth, as enshrined in the annual crime statistics, did not altogether accord with Mr Chubb's estimate, that was not his fault. The forty or fifty indictable offences that went on record each year showed merely that in every barrel there would be found a rotten apple. And it was the chief constable's belief that apple rot was not endemic but an imported infection.

Thus, when he received an urgent message from London that an American gangster might be on his way to Flaxborough in order to commit a crime, Mr Chubb saw no reason to view it sceptically.

'As I understand these matters,' he explained to Inspector Purbright, 'the Americans — who are nice enough people, by and large — have allowed themselves to be imposed upon by a well organised criminal element.

The Syndicate — would that be the term they use?'

'It would,' confirmed Purbright, anxious not to waste time by questioning a possibly outdated expression.

'It seems to be a very professional affair, in a nasty way, of course, and the consequence is that crime over there has become big business.'

Purbright forbore from pointing out that this proposition was palindromic. He said instead: 'So I believe, sir.'

Mr Chubb was standing by the window in Purbright's office. The light fell on silvery hair, sleek but cut short. His face, half averted in contemplation of buildings opposite, was of that paradoxical solemnity so often characteristic of the man who has never really worried about anything in his life.

'This so-called Syndicate,' the chief constable continued, 'apparently employs assassins to further its interests. Yes, I know it sounds rather like medieval Italy, but there you are: these things do go on and we have to take a realistic view.

'Anyway, the long and short of the matter is that our worthy opposite numbers in New York have warned me officially that just such an assassin has been ordered to come to England — to Flaxborough, in fact: they were quite specific.'

Chubb paused.

'And with what object, sir?'

'Presumably,' replied the chief constable, looking at once judicious and regretful, 'in order to attempt the murder of someone or other.'

'A local person?'

'Ah, well, that we do not know, do we, Mr Purbright. I would prefer to think not, but our main concern must be to see that the would-be assassin is prevented from doing any damage to anybody, whoever they are.

'This' — Mr Chubb produced a teleprinted sheet — 'is a copy of the letter which the New York police received yesterday.'

Purbright rose but Chubb, crossing from the window, motioned him back into his chair and put the paper before him. The inspector, who was several inches taller than the chief constable, had long since learned to accept without false protest Mr Chubb's preference for standing.

'So they really do use expressions like these,' the inspector said when he had finished reading.

'What we should term thieves' argot, I suppose,' said Mr Chubb, knowledgeably.

' "Contract" is pithy, sir. A lawyer's word. Significant, perhaps, of the ever narrowing division between them and their clients.'

Chubb's regard of his inspector chilled momentarily but he made no comment.

'I don't need to ask if our New York friends take this seriously,' Purbright said. 'Obviously they wouldn't have passed it on otherwise. And the probability of its not being a hoax is strengthened by the mention of a specific place. An obscure and unimportant place. In the New York context, I mean, of course,' he hastily qualified. 'It's a circumstantial detail that stands out rather impressively from the Spillanery.'

'Oh, I don't think the genuineness of the warning is at issue, Mr Purbright.' Chubb had no idea what "Spillanery" might be but would as soon have asked as put on a pair of jeans. 'Our job is to act upon it as a matter of urgency.'

Purbright nodded earnestly. 'Of course, sir.' He reached for a note pad. 'You will have in mind some main lines of action?'

'Yes, but I would not wish to prejudice your own ideas at this stage, Mr Purbright. If you will tell me what they are, we may possibly save ourselves a certain amount of duplication.'

The inspector drew a line down the middle of the top sheet of the pad. 'You will have seen straight away that our problem can be divided into two parts,' he said. 'So I propose to adopt the same approach as must already have occurred to you.'

'Ah,' said the chief constable, in the manner of one commending perspicacity.

'It is, in fact, an X and Y problem, sir. Where X is the journeying criminal, the assassin or potential assassin, and Y the intended victim. If we could establish the identity of either one of these two unknowns, our task would be very much easier. You are thinking' — Purbright gave Chubb a wry smile — 'of quadratic equations, naturally. Not at all a bad analogy.'

The chief constable shrugged modestly and looked down to see if Purbright had written anything yet. One or two notes had appeared on the left of the dividing line.

'All we know about this man X', Purbright went on, 'is that he is probably an American citizen — probably, but not certainly; that he is a member of an organisation of some kind — again probably, although I suppose there may be freelance murderers available; and that he is likely to have chosen as inconspicuous a way of travelling as possible — as an ordinary tourist, in fact.

'Twenty or thirty years ago, such a man could not have come into Flaxborough without being noticed by at least a dozen people who would have started a chain reaction of gossip. Nowadays, I doubt if there are fewer than ten American visitors in the town at any one time between June and September.'

If Mr Chubb found this estimate surprising, he did not challenge it.

'It did occur to me,' he said, 'that one of your fellows ought to check the visitors' books at all the hotels. Twice a day, perhaps; there can't be very many.'

'Three, actually, sir. There has been a good deal of shrinkage in that area.'

'That should simplify things, then.'

'Yes, sir. At least we shall be able to discount the families and concentrate upon anyone who registers on his own. An assassin taking his wife and children along on his expense account doesn't sound very possible.'

'Or very ethical,' added the chief constable, who liked occasionally to lend support to Mrs Chubb's loyal contention that her husband had a dry sense of humour.

'There is always the slight hope,' said the inspector, 'that the man X has a bad enough record, or else sufficiently spectacular criminal associations, to justify his being picked up on the way here, preferably before he can get on a plane.'

'The immigration people are extremely diligent, I understand.'

'No doubt, sir. But sheer weight of numbers can defeat the most stringent precautions. I still have a sort of Rider Haggard sense of wonder when I read of all those grenades and sub-machine guns that passengers manage to lug aboard aeroplanes.

'Anyway, so much for the X factor. Unless, of course' — Purbright looked up inquiringly — 'you have a further line you'd like me to pursue?'

Mr Chubb examined the sleeve of his light grey worsted jacket. 'It all sounds rather pessimistic, Mr Purbright. A criminal who cannot be identified can scarcely be apprehended.'

'Very well put, sir. Now I can see how you arrived at the analogy of algebra. Let me just trace the argument for my own satisfaction — oh, and please pull me up if I go wrong.

'As we well know, quadratic equations are simply statements of the relationships that certain unknowns bear to one another and, either singly or in combination, to known factors of the same kind. The solution is obtained by manipulating these relationships until each unknown is isolated by cancelling the others out. Do I follow you, sir?'

Mr Chubb, wooden-faced, gave an almost imperceptible nod. He stole a glance at Sergeant Love who was doing something with papers on a table, but Love seemed totally absorbed in his task.

'The only facts — or reasonable assumptions — about X,' the inspector continued blithely, 'are that he is a criminal and an American citizen and bound for Flaxborough. Not much to work on. And, at first sight, we have even *less* information about Y. Only that he lives here.

'But now let me see if I can spot some of the conclusions you have reached by cross-fertilising, so to speak, these two unpromising sets of data.

'Firstly, sir, you will say that Y is almost certainly a criminal himself. Not in the sense of being a gangster, as the man hired to kill him is a gangster. But you would rightly be surprised if there were no criminality in his dealings, in his associations.'

The chief constable was frowning deeply. 'Perhaps you should explain your reasoning on that point, Mr Purbright.'

'Of course, sir. It is simply that the professional criminal does not resort lightly to murder.. It is a solution reserved for the rival, the traitor, or the incorrigible non-returner of favours. No honest man ever gets himself into any of these categories.'

'I see,' said Mr Chubb.

'I should guess that your second deduction,' Purbright went on, 'is that Y is, or has been, fairly successful financially. No petty profiteer would qualify for such an expensive execution. Also, we find in the warning letter the term "wheel", which, if I am not mistaken, is American vernacular for a person of substance and influence.'

'Indeed,' said the chief constable.

'The third point that will have struck you is the nationality of X's employers. They are almost certainly American. So if we decide to narrow our field of search to include only prosperous or recently prosperous people whom we think capable of using questionable business methods, and then look among them for somebody who has visited or had dealings with America, we might, I agree, be lucky and reach Y before X does.'

The chief constable remained in silent consideration for a while. Then he looked at his watch.

'I really must be getting along now, Mr Purbright; there's a meeting I have to attend at eleven. You'll do your best with this affair, won't you? It would not exactly redound to our credit if some scoundrel were able to walk into the town and calmly do away with one of our residents.'

At the door, he turned upon Purbright a faint, wintry smile. 'After all,' he said, 'this is not Dodge City.'

As if suddenly released from bondage by Mr Chubb's departure, Sergeant Love rose and crossed the office. 'Where,' he asked, 'did *he* hear about Dodge City?'

'Do not underestimate our chief constable, Sid. He is a good deal better informed than he pretends.'

'So what was all *that* about?' Love jerked his head in the direction of the door.

'A task for us.' Purbright picked up from his desk the copy of the New York message. 'If this is to be taken seriously.'

Love read. He emerged from behind the paper, shiny with boyish enthusiasm.

'It's the Mafia!'

'Well, it's certainly not the Federation of Women's Institutes.'

'I couldn't follow all that guff you were giving old Chubb,' Love said.

'It *was* rather confusing,' Purbright admitted, 'but shorn of the spurious mathematics I think it stands up. All I meant was that it may be easier to guess the intended victim and then try and protect him than to sift through a bunch of tourists for a would-be executioner.'

'Torpedo,' Love emended.

The inspector nodded. 'Good. I see you can be relied

upon to cut through any linguistic difficulties. Wheels, now. Could you compile a list of wheels, Sid?'

'Grafters, too?' inquired the sergeant.

Purbright gazed at polyglot Love with undisguised admiration.

'Bill Malley has a membership list of the Chamber of Commerce,' he said. He rummaged through a desk drawer. 'And here's a town council diary: names are in the front section. From those two you ought to be able to produce a bag of notables. Money-makers are those we want, especially the dodgy ones, the fast fortune experts. Never mind the O.B.E. queue and the third generation grocers; the people who get themselves into this sort of trouble usually call what they do either promoting or developing.'

Love's initial eagerness had begun to fade. 'I'm not sure that we have anybody in Flax you could call a big wheel. There are plenty of grafters, but it's just Cons Club back-scratching, most of it.'

'Where's that breadth of vision of yours, Sid? Lenny Palgrove didn't collect three cars and his own plane simply by scratching backs. Hall, the estate agent, left £180,000 in February. Old Scorpe's brother-in-law paid a quarter of a million for that pig farm at Gosby and he wouldn't know the difference between a mash trough and a combine harvester. Oh, come on! What about Councillor Crispin — Happy Harry? And whatsisname, the coroner's nephew, with his fifteen hairdressing saloons? These are good times, Sid. All Ai ask is that you record the chief beneficiaries. I'll do the short-listing.'

Love said he would do his best.

'Sergeant Malley will help you,' said the inspector. 'He can tell you things about this town that even I don't want to know.'

Chapter Twelve

In a corner of a first-class compartment of the nine thirty-five train from King's Cross to Brocklestone-on-Sea, calling at Flaxborough, sat a heavily-built man in a lightly-built suit.

The suit was coffee-coloured but when the man moved in his seat as he did occasionally to ease himself or to shift his view of the landscape, a faint violet sheen was noticeable. The material seemed to contain a lot of silk: it looked slippery and inclined to drape.

The man's face was melancholy, plump-jowled, shinily-shaven yet with a residual darkness round cheek and chin that twenty shaves a day would not cure. His eyes, though slowed by tiredness, were watchful and very bright between lids that looked like rolls of uncooked pastry. He sniffed gently every few seconds. The sniff seemed somehow more than a mannerism, an unconscious habit. It was regularly timed and quite deliberate, as if the man had cultivated his sense of smell until it was a reliable monitoring device of self-preservation.

On the rack above the man's head was a medium-sized suitcase in blue figured hide with the monogram J.F.T. embossed in gold. A light-weight raincoat lay folded next to the case and on top of the raincoat was a black homburg.

The passenger's only other visible equipment was a sturdy, silver-mounted walking stick propped against the side of the carriage, and an unopened copy of the *Reader's Digest* on the seat beside him.

His invisible equipment included a United States passport in the inside breast pocket of his silky-looking suit. It proclaimed its carrier to be Joseph Fortescue Tudor, olive oil importer, born in 1906 in Syracuse, N.Y.

When the train drew into Flaxborough station, Mr Tudor seemed uncertain whether to alight or not. He had taken down his case and donned his coat and hat some time before, but now he stood at the carriage door and looked up and down the platform.

He beckoned a porter who was loading a trolley with parcels.

'Is this Flaxborough?' Mr Tudor's pronunciation of the name was not dissimilar from Sergeant Bast's.

Assured that it was, he tried to find the door handle.

'How do you open this thing?'

The porter came to his aid, puzzled that a gentleman travelling first class in the kind of hat which clearly confirmed his entitlement to do so should be beaten by so simple a problem.

Mr Tudor did not thank him verbally but handed him three pound notes. With fractional hesitation, the porter accepted the money. Clearly, a foreign notable: there was a trace of European accent in his otherwise American manner of speaking.

'Do you think you can find me a taxi?'

'I'll try, sir.' The porter, whose beard gave him the appearance more of an admiral than of a railwayman, went out into Station Square and hailed the cab of a cousin with whom he shared family loyalties and a small commission.

In the open space of the station booking hall, Mr Tudor seemed to diminish in height. It was his legs that lacked length; the body, though thickset, was powerful-looking and well proportioned.

As he emerged into the Square, he glanced to left and right with a swiftness that was almost lizard-like. He carried his suitcase in his left hand and kept the right in his raincoat pocket. Withered, perhaps, thought the porter, who had a gothic imagination; then he recalled the plump and hairy-backed but otherwise unexceptional fingers from which he had taken the £3.

'I want to go to a place called Church Close — Close? — is that right?' Mr Tudor held a scrap of paper for the driver to see.

'Put you down at the end, sir. Can't take a cab round the Close, but I'll get as near as I can.'

It occurred to the cab driver that his fare, being a foreigner, would appreciate seeing more of Flaxborough than St Anne's Place and Spoongate, which formed the shortest route to the parish church and its Close. He therefore contrived to include in his itinerary not only the whole length of Southgate and a quarter mile of Harbour Road but the more picturesque alleys of the Sharms district. Then, after a ten minutes wait at the Beale Street level crossing, he navigated a traffic-glutted West Row and emerged into the Market Place with its view of the great church of St Lawrence as a grand finale.

'Here you are, sir. Not far to walk from here. Just round the back of the church.'

A pity, he reflected, that his fare had missed so much scenery because of his habit of constantly looking back through the rear window.

The meter registered seventy-five pence. Mr Tudor, his melancholy expression unchanged, fished some crumpled notes out of his jacket pocket. He looked at them vaguely and handed them over as if disposing of an empty paper bag. The driver smoothed them out. There were four. He offered to hand one back. Mr Tudor flicked his plump fingers dismissively and turned away. He said nothing. His free hand was back home in that raincoat pocket.

Church Close was a crescent-shaped terrace of tall, narrow Georgian houses that faced the parish church across what once had been a graveyard but now was a broad, finely-turfed lawn. Each house was colour-washed in its own pastel shade, but white was the standard paint on doors and window frames. The glint of old brass, scrupulously burnished, shone here and there along the row from a knocker or a letter box. In the bright small-paned windows, reflections of the church's honey-coloured stone were rendered curiously twisted and globular by the irregularities of eighteenth-century glazing.

Mr Tudor stopped in front of the fifth door. He glanced back in the direction from which he had arrived, looked up sharply and briefly at the windows overhead, then knocked. While waiting, he stood at one side of the door, close to the wall, so that he could continue surveillance of the surrounding area.

The door was opened quietly but fully and with no hint of furtiveness.

'Good afternoon.'

The voice was gentle and precise, its note of interrogation unreservedly amiable.

Mr Tudor saw standing in the doorway a woman of still attractive middle age and recognised, although it was not until later that the resemblance was identified in his mind, one of those impeccably bred chatelaines he had seen from time to time in Hollywood films about the classier aspects of British life.

'Your name Lucia Teatime?'

'I am Miss Teatime. Lucilla, actually, but no matter.' No matter, either, she decided, that fate, through the agency of a romantically patriotic mother, had saddled her with Edith and Cavell as her middle names.

'Mack sent me. I'm Joe Tudor.'

'Mack,' she repeated delicately, half to herself. Then: 'Of course! Uncle Macnamara. He telephoned me. I am so sorry, Mr Tudor. Please come in.'

She stepped back, smiling a welcome. Mr Tudor, she noticed, had a rather curious way of entering a house; he did so sideways, very quickly for so solidly built a man, and with a final glance up and down the Close as if he was anxious not to miss some delayed companion.

'I am afraid that I have already had luncheon. Uncle

Macnamara gave me no indication of when I might expect you.'

Mr Tudor gave a grunt which Miss Teatime interpreted as a disavowal of interest in food. Perhaps he had eaten on the journey or even brought provisions of his own — hamburgers, or something of that nature, she surmised.

Miss Teatime led the way up the narrow staircase to her sitting-room on the first floor. Her guest was not the first visitor to observe on that brief but tortuous journey that time had dealt kindly (as one, a clergyman had expressed it to himself) with her nether parts, but he certainly was the first to remark on the fact.

'You got good legs, Looce.'

It was a statement: flat, gruff, unmotivated. Miss Teatime felt like an aging car, that had just been issued with another twelve months' roadworthiness certificate.

With one careful but unenthusiastic survey, Mr Tudor took in the details of the light and airy sitting-room, with its tall windows and its few choicely graceful pieces of furniture, and humped himself into an armchair. He had, Miss Teatime supposed, exhausted his compliments for that day.

'Would you care for a cup of coffee?' she asked, after giving him time to settle back, eyes half closed, in an attitude of stern introspection.

He considered, then nodded. 'Yeah. O.K.' It was a distinct concession.

When Miss Teatime returned with the coffee tray, she took a half bottle of whisky from a little hanging cupboard in the corner and set it by the cups.

Her glance of mute inquiry brought a 'Sure — why not?' from Mr Tudor. She laced his coffee with spirit and handed him the cup, then laced her own drink with a little coffee.

Both sipped without speaking for two or three minutes. She watched him with as much attention as delicacy permitted. In spite of his age, his mouth was full-lipped and sharply moulded — the mouth of a precocious boy. It contrasted strangely with the fallen, sallow cheeks and the whisker-shadowed jowls. She noticed his sniff.

'I do hope,' she said, 'that you have not caught a cold in this treacherous climate.'

He regarded her blankly. 'No. I'm O.K.'

'Prohibition,' said Miss Teatime, 'would be hopelessly impractical in a country with England's weather. I fear the population would be decimated in a fortnight were it not for these innocent prophylactics of ours.'

For the first time since his arrival, Mr Tudor gave sign of being able to respond to suitable social stimulus. A glint of happy recollection, of pride, shone in the nearly black eyes.

'Don't you knock prohibition, Looce,' he growled. 'Don't you ever knock that.'

Had Mr Tudor smiled for an instant? Miss Teatime was almost certain that he had. Then she saw that he was holding out his cup, apparently expecting her to refill it in mid-air. Rather lumber-camp-ish, she reflected, but perhaps intimating a desire to be friendly.

'Mack says you are doing all right in this, this Flaxborrow.'

'Oh, I manage quite happily,' responded Miss Teatime. 'This town is more restful than London, of course. And yet more interesting. I am not sure that I could explain the paradox to anyone from so stimulating a city as New York.'

Mr Tudor shrugged. 'We get our dead days.' He set his cup somewhat dangerously on the fat, chintz-dressed arm of his chair. 'So what is going for you here? How do you make your bread?'

'I have one or two little irons in the fire,' said Miss Teatime, modestly. 'What keeps me chiefly busy, perhaps, is my work as a charity organiser. I think I can claim some success in having put several good works on a business footing. The English, of course, respond eagerly to appeals of this kind, particularly when the welfare of animals is at issue. You would be surprised, Mr Tudor, to learn how much is contributed every year in this little town alone towards the provision of homes for the poor work-broken ponies of San Francisco.'

'Ponies?' Mr Tudor's upper lip drew away from his teeth in disbelief. 'Frisco?'

'Those street cars, you know,' explained Miss Teatime. 'The ponies haul on the cables beneath the roadway.' She frowned and shook her head. 'Perpetual darkness, I understand.'

Mr Tudor stared at her ruminatively for a moment, then, seemingly having decided not to risk making himself look foolish by labouring whatever subtle British joke had been intended, he said:

'My cousin Dino's boy, Johnnie, once ran all the Santa Clauses on the West Side.'

This was the longest speech Mr Tudor had made so far.

Miss Teatime smiled. 'Quite a coincidence, is it not, that you should have a charity organiser in your own family.'

'They used to call him Johnny Ding Dong,' said Mr Tudor, sadly.

Miss Teatime sensed that she had strayed into an area of bereavement. She changed the subject.

'Is Uncle Macnamara still making a name for himself in the merchant banking world? We had time only for a few fleeting pleasantries over the telephone.'

'He's doing great,' her visitor confirmed, suddenly stirred into something like animation. 'I tell you something, Looce. He has no problems, that Mack. Everything legitimate.' Mr Tudor nodded, pursing his full lips.

'*Everything*?' The first syllable was delicately stressed.

'Sure. No shakedowns. No whorehouses any more. No muscle.' A fat, hair-backed forefinger rose and wagged from side to side. 'Just real estate and stocks. Jeez, that office, Looce! Like a church. I tell you — a church!'

'Ah, yes: a man of parts,' declared Miss Teatime, adding, in silent parenthesis, *Mostly private.* Aloud, she asked:

'And what brings you to Flaxborough, Mr Tudor? It is not purely a social visit, I understand.'

'Business.' It sounded distasteful to him. 'Family business. Trouble maybe. I hope not.'

'Oh, dear. Do you suppose I might be of assistance?'

He considered a moment, then gave an extra loud sniff and leaned forward in his chair. He addressed himself less to Miss Teatime than to the palms of his hands, which he held before him and closely scrutinised.

'The word comes to my family from a good customer, who happens to be a cop, that some enforcement is going to get done that it looks like nobody knows about. And where? In Britain, for God's sake.' He glanced up, scowling. 'Right here in this village.'

'Town,' murmured Miss Teatime, loyally, but Mr Tudor was looking at his hands again and flexing them, deaf to so trivial an amendment.

'If what we hear is right,' Mr Tudor continued, 'it is the worst sort of business. The worst. Like the President says, this Anglo-American thing is O.K. Ask any of our men of honour back home. Men of respect. You know what I mean? They don't want this thing bust up just because some crazy button man thinks he can make a hit over here like it was Hoboken. What does he want, this fink? That every guy with a U.S. passport should get frisked?'

Mr Tudor's sudden volubility was impressive after the initial difficulties of their conversation. Miss Teatime hastened to show herself sympathetic.

'How pleasant it is in this cynical age,' she exclaimed, 'to hear that the cooperation of our two countries is valued by honest men.'

Her guest frowned. 'That I did not say, Looce. I said men of honour.'

'Ah, yes. Of course.' By offering at that moment a box of small cigars, Miss Teatime covered as best she could what she admitted to herself had been a gauche confusion of terms.

Mr Tudor said he did not smoke, but would like more coffee. She poured him another cup and lit a cigar for herself. He looked on with disapproval.

'I gain the impression,' she said, 'that the ladies in that family of yours do not smoke.'

'Years ago,' said Mr Tudor, 'I found my little sister Teresa in our momma's closet smoking a cigarette. I put that cigarette out. So. Just here.' He turned his head a little and pointed to a spot just below his left ear. 'She still has the mark.' He nodded. 'But she don't smoke.'

'Family affection does not run quite so strongly in this comparatively effete society,' observed Miss Teatime. 'Tell me, though, Mr Tudor — do you have any children of your own?'

She had scarcely completed the question when a wallet was being opened by stubby but surprisingly deft fingers and two photographs offered for her approval. The first pictured a sullen-faced man in his early thirties, with bold, very dark eyes and a fat neck that gave him that neanderthal hunch characteristic of the classic police 'wanted' poster.

'Giacomo,' said Mr Tudor, proudly.

'A very personable young man,' declared Miss Teatime. She put on a pair of glasses and looked more closely. 'Dear me, what a dangerous place to have received an injury.' She indicated a thin white scar from the corner of Giacomo's right eye to his upper lip.

'Kids!' expostulated the fond parent. 'Would you believe Jimmy did that falling off the can when he was four?'

Miss Teatime, who knew a razor slash when she saw one, would not, but she was too polite to say so. She inquired instead: 'And what is your son's choice of profession?'

'Olive oil importer.'

The second photograph was a little out of focus, but again the dark, challenging eyes of the Tudor family were immediately noticeable.

'Vittorio was going to be a priest.'

'Indeed?' Miss Teatime examined the well-fed, petulant face of the younger brother, with its hair-line moustache, reminiscent of dance halls in the 'thirties, and diagnosed a surfeit of maternal admiration and pasta. She guessed that whereas Giacomo probably operated in the protection sector, Vittorio's speciality would be either drugs or prostitution.

'He has a certain spirituality of countenance,' she said. 'Tell me, then: what vocation lured him from the seminary?'

'You mean what's Vic's job? Well, I guess he's in the olive oil importing business.'

When Mr Tudor had, with a lingering look of fondness, pouched once more the pictures of his offspring, he walked to the window and looked sideways down into the Close, keeping flat in the shelter of the wall.

Miss Teatime watched his manoeuvre impassively, then tapped the ash from her cigar into a little china pomade pot decorated with very pale cornflowers.

'So you come to Flaxborough in the role of a peacemaker,' she said.

Mr Tudor gave this some thought as he edged away from the window. Suddenly he nodded.

'Yeah. Yeah, you could say that.'

'What do you propose to do if you succeed in finding this fellow countryman of yours who is intent on killing someone or other? In any case, how would you recognise him?'

A confident half-grin briefly replaced Mr Tudor's expression of mourning. He pointed with a forefinger to each eye.

'These I have used every day, every night, right from

the days of Big Al. They know what to look for, Looce.'

'And when they find him?'

Mr Tudor's shoulders raised slightly. 'He'll listen. He'll have respect. I think maybe he will go back with me. In respect for my family, you understand?'

'I am not yet quite clear,' Miss Teatime said, 'as to how you think I may help in this commendable mission.'

'Tonight I ring my brother in Miami Beach. He will know whatever has been found out back home. Most of all, we want the name of the contract. As soon as we get this name, you can help. The cops we do not want. You are respected. The contract is a wheel, so respected, right? You go to the guy and tell him get lost a few days in Sherwood Forest or Loch Lomond or some place while I do a fumigation job for him. O.K.?'

With which burst of loquacity, Mr Tudor took a final squint out of the window, put on raincoat and hat, picked up his case and his stick, and made for the stairs. He would be available, he told Miss Teatime, 'at the village inn', by which, it transpired, he meant Mr Maddox's imposing establishment on East Street, the Roebuck Hotel.

Chapter Thirteen

The Mackintosh-Brooke team could not be accused of tardiness in the mornings. When Edmund Amis entered the Floradora a few minutes before nine o'clock, Bernard's head appeared round the door of the wassail hall. 'Morning, Ed.' A quick, alert smile. Then the head was withdrawn. Amis almost fancied that he could hear something being jotted down on a note clip.

He looked on the floor. No mail.

'Morning.'

Peter had come into the entrance hall, spruce as a

television salesman.

'I have the post, if you'd like to see it,' Peter said. 'I simply wanted to make a sample assessment of your communication situation.'

Amis followed him to Hatch's personal office, which had been put at the team's disposal for the week. Julian was seated at the desk, getting what he called 'the gut feel' of some ledgers.

Julian looked up, greeted him briskly, and indicated with a nod the sheaf of letters at the other end of the desk.

The secretary drew up a chair and did his best not to look annoyed.

On top of the pile was a letter that had not been opened. It was addressed in crude, hand-printed capital letters to Hatch in person. The envelope was of poor quality. 'Flaxborough' had been spelled out twice; the original, cancelled, version looked more like 'Flaxburow.' The letter bore three stamps to make up the United States air mail rate; two were large representations in yellow and violet half-tone of the President. The postmark was New York, the date four days before.

'I assumed,' remarked Peter, who was about to leave again, 'that that was something private. But the telegram I did open: it is in my recollection that Mr Hatch was unspecific in relation to the confidentiality of telegrams.'

Amis read and sorted the letters first. The telegram was at the bottom. Amis read it slowly. He was conscious that Bernard was watching him as he did so. He and the others had probably discussed it. And no wonder, Amis reflected.

PHILADELPHIA DEAL CLOSED DOLLARS THREE EIGHT ZERO ZERO STOP NAKEDNUNS WITH COVER DISPATCHED TODAY STOP NOTE INCREASE REASON EXTRA COMMISSION BISHOP STOP DALLAS REPORT FALSE NO NUNS BELIEVE SUPPLY ENDED CERTAIN STOP PAICE

'Code?' The quiet, laconic question came from Bernard.

Amis shrugged. 'Some sort of joke, more likely.'

'Joke?' Bernard sounded to be naming an incredibly rare metal.

'We do have our wags in these parts,' said Amis, drily.

'But it was sent from America. From Newark, New Jersey, in point of fact.'

Amis checked. 'So it was. Well, that simply makes it more elaborate, that's all. I can't imagine that any of old Hatch's enterprises require a code.' He gave Bernard a look of mockery that was nearly, but not quite, good-natured. 'Hasn't your team learned yet that they like playing games in this town?'

'We have certainly encountered some pretty counter-productive attitudes.'

Amis smiled. He put the cablegram aside and collected together a number of invoices from that morning's post. He unlocked a drawer of the desk and took out a cheque book.

Both men busied themselves with their separate tasks. Conversation lapsed.

Hatch examined and brooded over the letter from New York for fully ten minutes. At one point, he seemed about to screw it into a ball and throw it in the waste basket. But instead he read it once again and looked carefully at the envelope.

'Eddie.'

Amis appeared at the half open door.

Hatch motioned him to the desk.

'What do you make of this?'

Amis turned the letter about in his hand before reading. It was a sheet of common wrapping paper, roughly torn into a square. The message was made up of pencilled capitals, irregular in size and shape, childishly formed.

'From some kid, is it?' Amis asked. He held the paper fastidiously, as if suspecting stickiness.

Hatch shook his head. 'Read it.'

Amis did so, aloud but very softly, halting and frowning at the least legible words and repeating a phrase here and there in an effort to make the message sound coherent.

He looked up. 'Do *you* know what it means?'

'No idea.' Hatch thoughtfully scratched the back of his neck, then looked at his finger nails and said: 'But I don't like it.'

Amis again examined the letter.

'Payments?' he queried. 'Behind in *what* payments?'

'How the hell do I know?' Hatch kept his voice low, but on the pale, paper-like cheek annoyance had suddenly printed a small patch of red.

'Do you know anyone in New York who could have some sort of grudge against you?'

'Of course I don't.'

'But somebody there knows your name, obviously.'

Hatch made mumbled reference to mailing lists, but his expression suggested thoughts that already had hastened ahead. He jabbed the air with his finger. 'Listen, does that bastard Crispin ever get over to the States?'

'Oh, come now . . .'

'Well, does he? I'm asking you.'

Amis shrugged. 'I very much doubt it. Anyway, would he threaten to murder you just because of some trivial neighbourhood jealousy?'

'Not so trivial as you might think,' Hatch murmured. He started. 'Murder me? What do you mean, murder?' He grabbed back the letter.

Amis pointed to a line.

' "Hit," ' Hatch read out. ' "You are going to get hit." Somebody's threatening to beat me up. Nothing there about murder.'

There was a pause.

'Well, is there?' Hatch persisted.

Amis gave a nervous little laugh. 'Perhaps I've been

reading too many gangster stories. You could be right. I hope so. But "hit" does happen to be an American euphemism for kill. I thought you'd know that.'

Hatch scowled. 'There are so many damn silly expressions nowadays.' He stared at the letter. 'Oh, to hell with it. Some bloody lunatic . . .'

The paper was gathered suddenly into Hatch's bony fist. Amis gripped his arm.

'No. I think you ought to take it seriously. Just in case.'

Hatch looked at him, then slowly relaxed his fingers. The balled letter dropped to the desk, rolled a few inches, and began jerkily to expand as if taking quick little breaths of relief.

After a while, Hatch smoothed out the letter and read through it once more.

Amis watched him.

'I'd take it to the police, if I were you,' he said quietly.

'You think so?' Hatch did not raise his eyes.

'I do.'

Inspector Purbright did not tell Arnie Hatch in so many words that he was glad that afternoon to see him and his letter in combination. One does not, after all, congratulate the recipient of a threat to murder. But he did feel a sense of relief that at least the prospective victim had now been identified. At the same time, he was not a little pleased, privately, to reflect that Hatch had been one of his own three favourite candidates.

'Has anyone ever threatened you before, Mr Hatch?'

'Never.'

'You have never been — how shall I say — subjected to pressure? In hopes of getting money out of you, I mean.'

'Only by people I owe it to.'

Purbright acknowledged with a smile the businessman's joke. Hatch looked at him impassively. 'I suppose you mean blackmail, do you?'

'It's a generally understood term, Mr Hatch.'

'Aye, well, if this letter's blackmail, it's a funny way of going about it. According to my private secretary, it just says I'm going to get done in. No ifs. No how much. The chop.'

Purbright mentally noted the privacy of the secretary. He tried out my private sergeant. No good. Not Sidney Love. He said to Hatch:

'The letter refers to your being behind in certain payments, sir. It is, in fact, a dunning letter. Now, I don't suggest for a moment that physical assault — much less murder, as implied here — is a tolerable form of debt collecting, but if you do owe money to someone you must tell me.'

Hatch waved the suggestion away impatiently. 'No, no, no. Nothing outside the ordinary business commitments. Bills come in, they get paid, and that's that.'

'This,' said Purbright, 'is certainly not an invoice in the accepted sense. It would seem to refer to dealings outside your normal commercial field.'

'Never mind what it refers to, inspector. It's a threat, and a damned nasty threat. All I want to know is what you're going to do about it.'

'Everything we can, sir, obviously. But you can help us in the first place by answering some questions. For example, I should like to know to what extent you are acquainted with America.'

'I make the trip occasionally. Not often. It's necessary for anybody who wants to keep up with trends in club management.'

'Las Vegas — places like that?'

'That's right.'

Purbright flicked through his meagre geographical knowledge for a suitably inept suggestion. He turned up the blameless domicile of his wife's cousin, a lecturer at Princeton.

'Metuchen?' he prompted with a man-of-the-world smirk.

Hatch's 'I'll say' was a low-keyed *ça va sans dire* that immediately populated that unexceptionable borough with a colourful horde of gamblers, saloon keepers and pimps. It convinced the inspector that Hatch's connections with the transatlantic vice industry, if he had any, would be at second or third remove.

'If you have never put yourself under an obligation,' Purbright said, 'during one of your visits to America, it is difficult to see why you should now receive a letter of this kind.'

'Aye, it *is* difficult,' said Hatch, in obtuse agreement. He was beginning to suspect in Purbright a certain deficiency of respect. He leaned forward and added sharply: 'But I *have* received it, haven't I?'

Purbright got up and walked to the window and back. He stretched and then sat again, not in his chair but on the corner of his big, dilapidated desk. He gazed thoughtfully at Hatch.

'Very well,' he said, 'we'll disregard the part about arrears of payment. You say there have been no loans, no favours, no promises. Perhaps the idea was a blind of some kind, an attempt to obscure the writer's motives.'

Hatch gravely conceded that possibility.

Purbright continued:

'So we must try and think of somebody who might want to harm you for reasons other than financial ones. Revenge, perhaps. Jeolousy. There aren't all that many, sir, once money is excluded.'

Hatch pretended to consider while he looked round Purbright's office. It was quite a big room but apart from the desk it was furnished with only a couple of chairs, two filing cabinets and a cheap-looking table against the wall opposite the window. The carpet was much worn, of an indeterminate colour and pattern, and so economical in area that the comfort of standing on it could be enjoyed by only one person at a time. The walls were painted in a cream gloss and were bare except for a large, age-yellowed poster setting out the regulations and tolls applicable to Flaxborough market in 1947.

Hatch completed his survey of the office with a speculative stare at its central occupant. A long-legged, easy-going fellow who probably had never scraped more than fifty quid into one pile in his life. Likeable enough, perhaps, but no drive. With that funny flax-coloured hair, he looked like some big Viking who'd missed the boat home and gone soft.

'Any ideas?' prompted the Viking.

Hatch massaged a bony thumb and pouted in shrewd thought. 'We've all given offence to somebody or other at some time in our lives. I can't think of any particular person, though.'

'An American, perhaps?'

'No. Not an American. I don't know any bloody Americans.'

'You sound cross, Mr Hatch. I'm sorry, but you really must try and be patient for your own sake.'

A sigh, a gesture at once perplexed yet conciliatory. 'I didn't want to make a fuss in the first place. We're just wasting our time with this.'

'I hope we are, sir. And we must try and minimise the waste by being absolutely frank.'

Hatch worked this out. Then he said:

'You're taking this seriously — this stupid letter? All right, I can see you are. Then can we start the frankness by you telling me what you know and I don't?'

After brief consideration, Purbright nodded.

'Very well, sir. We've already had a warning from the New York police that someone over there might be planning to come to England — to Flaxborough specifically — in order to attack a person living here.'

'Me, you mean?'

'No details were given. The only name mentioned was

that of the town itself. I'm relieved in one sense that you've been threatened directly. At least we know whom to protect.'

'Are you confident you *can* protect me? That's the point, isn't it.'

'Very much so. We'll do everything we can, naturally, in a general sense. But the job would be a hundred times simpler if we knew who would *want* to attack you. Surely, Mr Hatch, this must be a case of personal vindictiveness, personal vengeance. I am not going to ask you again if money is involved. You say not. So the man we must watch for is either someone who considers himself mortally offended by something you have done or failed to do — someone of your acquaintance, in fact — or else a wandering maniac who happens to have picked your name out of his loonie hat. Once again I must ask you to try and recall any incident, however unsavoury or personally embarrassing, and irrespective of what you might consider calls on your loyalty, which could account for this threat.'

'How do you mean, calls on my loyalty?' asked Hatch at once. He had been listening sullenly but, Purbright supposed, with clear enough understanding. His challenge of this one phrase suggested apprehensiveness rather than doubt of its meaning.

'Loyalty, for example, to a married woman whom one happens to have seduced.'

Hatch slowly leaned back in his chair. His mouth, tightening, grew pale, bloodless.

'Or an unmarried one, for that matter, sir,' persisted Purbright, with matter-of-fact cheeriness.

There was silence for several seconds. Then Hatch's voice, very quiet but harsh, a scratchy nib of a voice.

'You'd better be able to offer proof of that suggestion, inspector. I'm warning you.'

'Oh, come now, sir. One warning at a time. You must not take personally these little guide lines I am trying to give you. Wronged husbands can be very dangerous — more dangerous, probably, than thwarted creditors, even. With respect, I think I would rather sacrifice — and in confidence, at that — some small part of the blamelessness of my reputation, than put at risk a large part of my expectation of life.'

The inspector met levelly the cold glare of Hatch's half-closed eyes.

'Do you go to church, inspector?'

'Not habitually, sir. No.'

'I thought not.'

Hatch stood. His face was grave. With meticulous dignity, he put on the black banker's hat. In that moment, Purbright thought, he looked like the late Mr Justice Avory, about to curl his lizard's tongue around his favourite food, a nice death sentence.

But all Hatch said, before he turned curtly and left the office, was: 'Good afternoon.'

On the next occasion of Purbright's seeing him, he was to say even less.

Chapter Fourteen

The medieval banquet was due to begin at half-past eight. The Mackintosh-Brooke team had decided that it should be their targeted dig for that day; banquet-viability was clearly an important ingredient of the profit mix of Floradora Enterprises.

Peter had zeroed in on the catering situation. Julian tackled costings. Bernard prepared to compile a time and motion profile.

In the club kitchen, Peter inspected the arrangements which were already well in hand. The main feature of the meal had been thawing out since the previous day. It was a great tray of deep-frozen battery chickens. These were "ye Capons". They would be sprayed with a brown crisp-from-the-oven aerosol stain and given fifteen minutes' cooking in a pressurised steam tank before being placed on individual platters of simulated pewter, stuck with a dagger apiece, and borne on rough-hewn timber trolleys into the Wassail Hall.

A busy, beady-eyed little man in a white coat was supervising the cutting of thirty or forty loaves into three-inch hunks. Peter addressed him.

'One whole chicken each. Is that right? A whole chicken?'

'Oh, aye. They get a good go at the grub. Well, that's what they pay for, isn't it?' The man cuffed the ear of a youth who, staring at the stranger, had dropped some bread. The boy scampered after the rolling loaf and stopped it with a deftly extended boot.

'Anyway,' the man added, 'it wouldn't be medieval if it wasn't whole, would it?'

'I wish,' said Peter, 'to have a clear picture of the consumption-participation ratio. What items are being pipelined at this moment in time in addition to the chickens?'

'What else are they going to get, d'you mean? Well, there's the bread, isn't there? They used to get veg when we started the thing, but the buggers got to chucking them about. Can you imagine what it was like going round afterwards and scraping cold cauliflower off of the bloody wainscotting? So its just bread now and like it. Until the Nellies go round with the oranges, of course.'

'Nellies?'

'They're the hostesses, got up in their Nell Gwyn sets. It's them who serve the sack before they do the orange round.'

'I'm sorry to ask so much explanation-wise, but sack . . ?'

His guide plucked Peter's sleeve and led him to a big, white-enamelled cylindrical vessel, set in a corner of the kitchen. The cylinder had two taps. Next to it were shelves, stacked with metal tankards.

'Twenty gallons of Spanish plonk in there. Kept at eighty degrees till we want it. Thermostat, see?' He pointed. 'Run off a pint apiece, bung in a few of them raisins, and bob's your uncle. Mulled sack. Smashing.' He reached down a tankard. 'Here — have a dollop, and see if it doesn't give you a touch of the old hey nonnies.'

Peter took refuge behind his note clip. 'Later perhaps,' he said. 'We have to prioritize right now.'

'Suit yourself, squire,' said the man. He replaced the tankard and wiped, with every appearance of cheerful indifference to rebuff, his nose upon the sleeve of his Wassail Master's coat.

At Fen Street police headquarters, Inspector Purbright was reading through some hastily compiled reports upon recent arrivals from abroad at the town's hotels. The four plain clothes men entrusted with the task had been instructed to arouse neither resentment nor suspicion, but simply to note names and places of origin, to learn the object of the visit where this could be done tactfully, and to gain from off-hand gossip with proprietors and staff what impression they could of the character and bearing of their guests.

Not a very scientific method, Purbright admitted to himself, but the best that could be devised at short notice and having regard for the tourists' right to freedom from harrassment.

After noting that seven of the twelve names in the collection were of members of a single delegation from Turkey, all agricultural students, Purbright turned with relief to the more manageable remainder.

The most sinister by repute of this quartet the inspector felt able to eliminate at once. The chamber maid informant of Detective Constable Boggan said that the gentleman, a bearded Australian who wore a clerical collar, had asked her very earnestly if she would help him with his photography. Assassins, Purbright reasoned confidently, were by nature men of severely limited and arid hobbies.

All the other three recently registered travellers were American.

Two, a middle-aged man and wife from Tucson, were hopeful, according to confidences they had very freely and pleasantly dispensed, of establishing Flaxborough as the birthplace of one of their eighteenth-century forebears. Great encouragement in this enterprise had been given, apparently, by a present-day Flaxborough resident, Miss Lucilla E.C. Teatime, director of an organisation named Famtrees.

The Tucson pair seemed, on the face of it, innocent enough. Police Constable Braine had kept an eye on them during the past couple of days and had detected no deviation from the established tourists' round of harbour, church, guildhall, parish registry, municipal museum, Ann Boleyn Tea Room and Ye Olde Yew Tree Inn (the staircase banisters in which were supposed to have been fashioned from the quarter-staff of Little John,) other than a couple of calls at Miss Teatime's office at 31 St Anne's Gate.

Consulted on the point, Sergeant Love said that torpedoes, or button men, were not trained in elaborate techniques of deception. His understanding was that a pulled-down hat brim or a mid-day edition of a sporting newspaper was as much cover as most of them would deem sufficient.

'And they don't bring their wives along, I imagine,' said Purbright, harking back to the earlier expressed theory of his own.

Love agreed, although he felt that it would be rash to rule out the possibility that the lady from Tucson was what he called 'another hood in drag'.

'And so,' said the inspector, 'we are left with this

Mr Tudor, of New York.' He quickly re-read Constable Burke's notes and added: 'Who also appears to be on a hunt for ancestors.'

'Oh?'

'Burke says he followed him round the town yesterday and saw him call at a house in Church Close. Number five. Our Lucilla's, in fact.'

'The house — not her office?'

'The house, yes. So perhaps he's a friend, not a client. I must ask her. In the meantime' — Purbright passed Burke's report to the sergeant — 'I'd like you to get the name and description wired to Immigration for checking with the people in America, if you wouldn't mind.'

'Where is he staying?'

'At the Roebuck.'

Love made a mock-posh grimace. He glanced through the report on Tudor while walking to the door.

'Oh, and Sid . . .'

The sergeant turned.

'If anyone wants me during the next hour or so, put a call through to me at that club of Hatch's will you? I'm going to have a look round.'

Love acknowledged this announcement with another piece of face-pulling from his repertoire: a contortion supposedly expressive of horrid knowingness.

Five minutes after the sergeant's departure, Purbright descended the rickety iron staircase which still, though nearly a century old, was the only connection between the upper offices and the now more-or-less modernised ground floor of the police building. He went out through a side door into the transport yard.

Two cars stood in their bays. For a moment he deliberated which would be less unreliable. Then he changed his mind altogether, walked out into Fen Street and took the opposite direction to that which would have led him past Jubilee Park to the Floradora.

He crossed East Street, turned right, then left into

St Anne's Gate.

The doorway of number 31 was graced with flanking columns and a fine Georgian fanlight, features that had survived oddly but with dignity the construction of a flashy shop window on either side.

The door stood open. Purbright climbed steep, uneven stairs to the first floor.

Three doors faced the broad landing. Their painted panels gleamed in the sunshine that shafted down from a tall, many-paned window set high in the stair well. The middle door was marked Private. On the door to its left was a small metal plate inscribed: Flaxborough and Eastern Counties Charities Alliance, Registered Office. The door on the right bore a polished oak panel, about a foot square, with wording painted in black Gothic script. Purbright went up to it.

FAMTREES — Genealogical Consultants.

He knocked and after some delay was bidden enter.

'My *dear* inspector!'

The pleasure his appearance had occasioned in the lady hurrying across the big, almost bare room with hand outstretched in greeting was patent. He allowed himself to be ushered to a chair beside the large table where Miss Teatime appeared to have been working on a chart of some kind.

'A new departure for you, surely,' said Purbright, looking round the room with what Miss Teatime recognised to be courteous interest, as distinct from officious nosiness.

'One must diversify, as they say nowadays.' She cleared a space among the sheets of paper on the table. 'Would you care for a cup of tea?'

'I should, indeed. Thank you.'

Miss Teatime went out through a door labelled ARCHIVES. Purbright supposed it to lead to the room sandwiched between Famtrees and the Charities Alliance.

He recalled an occasion a couple of years before when he had sat in the Alliance office and noticed a corresponding door. That door had been marked BOARD ROOM. He listened. There emerged sounds of china being assembled on a tray and the filling of a kettle. A versatile compartment, Purbright reflected.

'Have you,' Miss Teatime asked him when they both had taken a first sip of tea and relaxed, 'come here on a professional matter?'

'I have,' replied the inspector.

'Your profession or mine?'

'Put it this way. I have come to consult you.'

'You will not regret it,' declared Miss Teatime. She beamed at him, then began sorting among the papers on the table until she uncovered a pack of cheroots. 'Purbright is a splendid old name. We might get you back to the Hospitallers of Saint John, with moderate good fortune. Or have you' — she peered past the flame with which she was lighting a cheroot — 'a preference for less piratical antecedents?'

'I should like a drop of whisky in this tea,' Purbright said.

Her laugh was immediate, buttercup-bright. From behind a battered copy of *Burke's Peerage* on a shelf beside her she drew a half-bottle of Highland Fling.

The inspector held out his cup.

'Flourishing, is it — your consultancy?' he inquired.

'It does seem that I have brought to light a long-felt want,' Miss Teatime said earnestly. 'To be able to give people a sense of *belonging* is a reward in itself, of course, but I do have to make a nominal charge, alas. As you may imagine, Rouge Dragon would be down on me like a ton of bricks were I to follow natural instinct and waive the fee.'

'Yes, I suppose he would.'

'But in fact people are very happy to pay for what I term the comforting shade of a nice family tree. Mrs

Hockley, for instance — ah, and this is in strict confidence, naturally, inspector — Mrs Hockley, from Cadwell Avenue, whose husband was an alderman and a dipsomaniac, I can now only describe as a transfigured woman.'

'Indeed?'

'Oh, yes. I was able to establish a strong trace of Marlborough there. If we all enjoyed our rights, Mrs Hockley would have her feet up at Blenheim at this very moment.'

Purbright said it was a small world.

'She entertains no bitterness, fortunately. A less philosophical lady would be importuning the Churchill Trustees. One has to be *so* wary in the lineage business. A lady from Snowden Avenue, I remember, whose connection with the House of Hanover seemed a distinct possibility, took it upon herself to write some *very* disrespectful letters to our dear Queen. I had to veer her line a bit towards the Stuarts in order to persuade her to desist.'

'My errand this afternoon,' observed Purbright, 'is to do with the house of Tudor, Miss Teatime. And in no genealogical sense, I'm afraid.'

Her bright, shrewd eyes were still. After a pause, she murmured: 'A lamentably disreputable dynasty. Libertines, head-choppers and bigots, one and all. I never advise a client to seek relationship with *them*.'

'The client I am talking about did not call here, but at your house in the Close. He is an American gentleman and his name is Joseph Tudor. I do not think that he has come all this way to claim kinship with Henry the Eighth.'

Miss Teatime regarded Purbright with a hint of sad reproof. 'You have had this man followed, have you not?'

'To anyone but you' — Purbright sniffed the aroma of his laced tea appreciatively — 'I would say that he has been kept under surveillance as a matter of routine. But I hope you give me credit for regarding surveillance and routine as mutually exclusive terms.'

'Would that more policemen were of like mind.'

Purbright made the smallest of bows.

'The fact is that we are a little nervous of Americans in Flaxborough at the moment. Ungenerous of us, perhaps, but there has been talk of murder.'

'By someone from the United States?'

'The warning came from New York, certainly. It's only sensible to heed it.'

'Naturally,' agreed Miss Teatime. She was looking thoughtful.

'This Mr Tudor,' she said after a pause, 'is not, as I think you surmised, a client. He is a friend of a friend. More accurately, an acquaintance of an acquaintance.'

Purbright waited a few seconds. 'Do you know anything about him?'

'Not a great deal.' She set straight a couple of the papers before her, then looked blandly out of the window.

'Why did he come to Flaxborough?'

'Family business, it seems, inspector. He was not specific on that point and of course I did not press him.'

'Then what was his object in calling upon *you*, Miss Teatime?'

'In part to pay the respects of a mutual acquaintance, as I have intimated already. Also, to inquire the whereabouts in this locality of a catholic church. It appears that Mr Tudor is of the Popish persuasion.'

Something stirred in Purbright's memory. 'Did he by any chance,' he asked, 'seem interested in nunneries?'

Miss Teatime frowned. 'I cannot say I received that impression. However, Mr Tudor obviously is a devout man. It well may be that he likes to sample the native cloisters when he travels abroad.'

The inspector tried to decide whether Miss Teatime's skittishness was intended as compliment or camouflage. Then another explanation occurred to him. If she did have serious misgivings concerning Tudor, she would not be so unsubtle as to express them directly. But she knew how to employ flippancy — a kind of verbal wink — to give warning of something she was too astute to acknowledge.

'This friend of yours who introduced him — I suppose you feel you can depend on his judgment?'

'He is a merchant banker,' announced Miss Teatime.

Purbright caught a certain nuance of embarrassed apology, or thought he did. 'Never mind,' he said.

'Mr Tudor has substantial financial interests in his own country,' added Miss Teatime, in a happier tone. 'I understand he is extremely influential. His compatriots have even made him a member of the Committee for the Re-election of the President.'

The inspector made a soundless whistle of awe. 'Have you plans to see him again?' he asked.

'Only very briefly,' said Miss Teatime. 'He promised to call at five o'clock to collect a dinner ticket he commissioned me to obtain.'

'Dinner ticket?'

'A banquet ticket, to be precise.'

'The Floradora?'

'The same. Mr Tudor feels that he cannot let pass the opportunity of gnawing a bone or two across the centuries. He is a perfervid traditionalist.'

Purbright considered. 'These tickets . . .'

'Are difficult to come by,' asserted Miss Teatime quickly. 'I often wonder at the eagerness of people to part with their money in return for a blend of nostalgia and dyspepsia.'

'A distressing thought. But I was wondering if you might repeat for me the favour you did Mr Tudor.'

Her face twinkled with pleasure. 'My dear Mr Purbright, if I could not oblige a friend in so small a matter, what would be the use of my having been appointed an official agent?' She opened a drawer. 'How many tickets would you like?'

'One,' said Purbright. He took out his wallet. 'And I should appreciate a receipt, if you would be so kind. The lucky gourmet I have in mind is a policeman and he will be there on duty.'

Chapter Fifteen

Behind a door inscribed "Tiring Roome of Ye Serving Wenches", time-and-motion-studying Bernard watched the female employees of Mr Arnold Hatch good-humouredly zipping one another into the seventeenth century. The Flowers obviously enjoyed banquet nights. As soon as they had been successfully compressed into their Nell Gwyn costumes, they would be inspected by Mr Hubbard, the Wassail Master, and each issued with the regulation tumbler of gin that was calculated to render her merrie and amenable to such medieval liberties as the guests might reasonably be expected to take during the festivities.

Somebody recalled with a giggle that one former Flower, dismissed after only a week for adopting an uncooperative attitude, had compared this favour with the rum ration that preceded going over the top in the first world war. There was a chorus of derision from the others. They assured Bernard that the girl quoted had been freaky and 'a real wet'.

In Hatch's office, Julian sat amidst account books, bank statements, receipts, counterfoils, invoices, tax forms and Customs requisitions; contented as a sheep in a clover crop. A plate of sandwiches lay untasted on the desk beside him. He had been working steadily for nearly eleven hours. Upon his smooth, tanned, quite handsome face, was the faintest of smiles. He believed he had verified out a meaningful and on-going misapplication of accountancy techniques.

Julian was much too preoccupied with his task to notice the small sounds made by somebody entering in a tactful and considerate manner the next room along the corridor.

This was a sitting room of sorts, that had been included in the original plan of the club on Mrs Hatch's suggestion so that when her husband should suffer his heart attack (Mrs Hatch awaited this lamentable event with fatalistic acceptance, for she was convinced that coronaries were contiguous to prosperity and she did not want to be poor again) medical aid might be rendered in more elegant surroundings than an office. Mr Hatch, however, had not guessed this consideration and had allowed the room to become a repository for discarded, if expensive, odds and ends: fishing rods, a tape recorder, the first three volumes of the *Cyclopaedia of the Occult* (an Astounding Opportunity), an eight-hundred guinea Olson and Morgan hammerless twelve-bore, a (Genuine Swiss) fondu bowl, and an undersea harpoon gun that had been part of the preparations for a Caribbean cruise, subsequently abandoned.

Peter left the kitchen at eight o'clock and took up a position in the Wassail Hall from which he could identify further opportunities for larding into the catering system an optimal element of motivation.

The sounds of minstrelsy were already being produced in the gallery by Roy Hubbard and his Rockadours in a warming up session. Roy, a Flaxborough electrical contractor and the younger brother of the Wassail Master, had developed a species of electronic lute. It made a noise, when suitably amplified, like the snapping of two-inch steel cables in Alpine valleys.

'Whe-e-ere are the Yo-ho-men, the Yo-ho-men of-Vingland?' inquired Roy at full belt. He looked as if the question had been worrying him for a very long time.

'Wah wah wa-wa-wah,' the Rockadours replied,

non-committally. There were three of them. They wore gold lamé riding breeches, heralds' coats in pink and purple checks, and perky Robin Hood hats. All were chewing.

The first diners to arrive were a party of twenty members of Hambourne Women's Institute, brought on a chartered bus. The evening was to be a special treat, for which they had rehearsed by holding a competition for a piece of tapestry representing "What I Like Best About the Middle Ages". The winner had worked in wool a fair copy of as much of The Rape of the Sabine Women as she could get done in time. The judging committee had not been entirely happy about the latitude of interpretation, but failure to reward Mrs Goshawk's wool-matching sense and uniformity of stitch, to say nothing of the fact that she was the wife of the only doctor in the village, would have been unthinkable. So here she was, at the head of her party's table, listening happily to such scraps of high-spirited conversation as were not swept down-board by Roy Hubbard's band.

Another early arrival was Detective Constable Burke. A police car brought him out from town and set him down at a point on Hunting's Lane some two hundred yards from the club. After completing the journey on foot, he slipped into the shelter of shrubs that bordered the Floradora drive and formed a hide from which the entrance could be kept under observation. His instructions were to await the appearance of the man from the Roebuck Hotel whom he had been following the previous day. If the man had not arrived by half past eight, Burke was to take a seat at the festive board and continue to keep watch in case Tudor turned up late.

But Tudor was not late. At twelve minutes past eight, a taxi drew slowly past Burke's bush. It was one of a number of cars that had turned into the driveway in close succession and were being delayed by some confusion in the parking area ahead.

Burke recognised the American at once. What he did not recognise was the fact that when Tudor leaned back, idly luxuriating in a yawn, he was actually taking in as much information through the gun turret slits of his seemingly closed eyes as if he had been staring as boldly — and incautiously — as Constable Burke.

The taxi stopped, started, stopped again. Burke remained in cover, watching through its rear window the outline of Tudor's hat against the floodlit face of the club, flaring in the dusk like an electric bouquet.

When the taxi reached the bay in front of the entrance doors, it was approached by what appeared at Burke's distance to be a huge turtle, waddling upright upon its back flippers. Burke hastened nearer but kept in the lee of a car. He saw that the figure was in fact a doorman in a Henry VIII costume, puffed to almost spherical proportions.

The doorman pulled open the taxi door and recited with neither enthusiasm nor punctuation:

'My lord and lady pray welcome to ye feast God save King Harry.'

For a moment, Tudor gazed admiringly at the spectacle of Gardener Todd, transfigured by doublet and stuffing. 'You the retainer or something?' he inquired gruffly.

'Yer wot?' glowered Todd. He was sensible of the vulnerability imposed by the obligation to 'ponce around in this get-up', as he put it.

Tudor leaned close, a pound note between two fingers. 'Get this door shut quick and waste the next guy's time a bit, O.K.?' He swung across to speak to the driver. As the door slammed, the taxi moved forward. It accelerated noisily towards a bend in the driveway and disappeared from view.

Constable Burke stood in a coma of puzzlement for a moment, then strode to the car that had just reached the head of the queue and was receiving the attention of a doorman suddenly and unaccountably enfeebled and hard of hearing.

Burke sternly informed the driver that he was a police officer requiring his immediate cooperation. The driver — a Mr Padstowe, who had brought his wife and sister-in-law all the way from Derby to be banqueted — was too bewildered to do anything but let his passengers be bundled out and himself enjoined to 'follow that taxi that was here a minute ago'.

'I'm not a fast driver, you know,' complained Mr Padstowe, defensively, when they drew up at the junction with the main road.

'It's not a fast taxi,' said Burke. He peered in both directions along Hunting's Lane. 'We'll try the way back towards town first.'

Mr Tudor, who was rather better at standing behind shrubs than was Constable Burke, watched Mr Padstowe's car disappear into the twilight. He then strolled slowly back to the Floradora, savouring the novel but pleasant mixture of the scents of mould and evening flowers and wood smoke that reminded him he was a very long way from Manhattan.

Two more coaches drew up. One disgorged some thirty members of the Chalmsbury Darby and Joan Club. From the other descended a miscellany of ticket holders from the Cambridge area. They stood in separate and irresolute groups until there appeared Gardener Joxy, disguised as an executioner. He waved his plastic axe in the direction of the club entrance and mutteringly adjured them to 'getfuknshiftedinfurfukngodsake'.

This message, though not receiving their literal understanding, was taken in good part, and Joxy's droll attire earned many a laugh and nudge from the new arrivals.

'Are you Henry the Eighth's lady-killer, then?' inquired one jocular old soul. Her companions squealed with delight.

'Gitfuknstuffed,' the headsman responded tightly through his mask.

The ladies grinned happily and moved on.

Mr Tudor mingled with them. For a man of solemn nature, he looked moderately pleased with life, but one felt that no degree of contentment would ever quite overcome his right hand's curious propensity for loitering in the neighbourhood of his left armpit, nor lull the practised watchfulness of his eye.

The proprietor of the Floradora, no lover of nostalgic junketting, was circulating from group to group in the more constrained atmosphere of the gaming-room. He was accompanied by his secretary. Mrs Hatch very seldom visited the club, unless her advice were sought on a change of décor; she insisted on calling it her husband's 'place of business' and gave the impression that she believed his presence there afforded him no more pleasure than if it had been an insurance office or a bank.

The two men stood at a slight distance from the roulette table. Hatch appeared contented, complaisant almost. Amis glanced about him restlessly. He looked apprehensive.

'To hell with Purbright,' said Hatch, quietly. 'What does he expect me to do — lock myself in the bloody lavatory?'

'He must have had some reason for asking you to stay at home this evening.'

'Reason, my arse. The more I think about this nonsense the more I'm sure that that bugger Crispin's behind it. And I'm not biting.'

Hatch nodded at a group of town councillors and their wives who were sitting close behind the wheel operator, primly self-conscious. The comparative novelty of gambling in Flaxborough was an attraction, certainly, but by no means a compulsion. Councillor Hillberry, for instance, looked about as dissipated as a grocer weighing bacon, while Mrs Nixon, wife of the vice-chairman, clutched her chips like dominoes and kept asking: 'Do I put one down now?' in a happy little bleat to which she neither received nor seemed to expect response.

The only really professional touch about the proceedings was the smirk of satanic superiority on the face of the operator. He was a young man employed during the day by the local gas board as a meter reader.

Only two Flowers were in the gaming-room, all the other hostesses having been mobilised for Nelly duty. These two were dealing to card games, but it was too early to attract full tables.

As Hatch and Amis loitered for a moment to smile upon dealer Marigold and her few communicants and wish them good evening, there entered through the doorway at the far side of the room a man whose calculated unobtrusiveness of manner set him apart at once from the other customers, all hugely aware of their exposure to iniquity.

It was Mr Tudor. In less than ten seconds, and with no betrayal of the slightest interest, his darkly hooded eye had registered every face in the room. Then he turned, and was gone.

By half past eight, practically every bench in the Wassail Hall was filled. Nellies had begun to push their serving wagons along the gangways. They picked up the tankards of mulled sack and reached across the guests from behind, simultaneously contriving, as a part of the entertainment which would long linger in the memory of those favoured, to poultice the right ear of every gentleman with a generous helping of bare bosom.

Peter observed this tactic. He made a jotting.

Permissiveness pivotal to hostess situation but check deniability.

Upon a raised dais in the centre of one side of the hall sat some thirty guests who had paid extra to share what the brochures called "The Baronial Board".

Their privileges included the wearing of articles of

medieval dress from the club wardrobe; a double quaffing quota that included a "draught of My Lord's Canary"; permission to belch and to match wits with the Jester; and the exclusive personal service at their table of Maid Marion. Behind this picturesque pseudonym bloomed buxom Mrs Roy Hubbard, dubbed by her husband's sole literate acquaintance 'the Last Lay of the Minstrel'.

Maid Marion sidled along the table, handing out daggers. She had already been round with wine. Some of the women looked apprehensively at the daggers; others looked even more apprehensively at Maid Marion, whose décolleté was almost navel-deep.

'Ho, there, wench!' called out a wholesale seedsman, wearing a surcoat over his lounge suit and determined to enter into the spirit of things. His companions made a few short, experimental noises of jocularity, then waited for further encouragement.

Maid Marion speared a capon from the trolley and slapped it on the seed merchant's platter. 'Pick ye bones out of that one, sirrah!' she cried.

Applause all round.

A senior clerk from the council highways department, gowned and capped in Chaucerian style, proposed that they 'fall to right heartily, gentles all!' His furiously blushing wife dragged at his sleeve and muttered 'Bert!' but it was clear that the infection had gained hold and would not now easily yield.

'To the dungeons with yonder varlet!' cried a quantity surveyor from North Gosby, whose intake of sack was beginning to react curiously with the five Martinis he had downed in the bar a little earlier in the evening. He pointed at a man in Richard III costume whose wife was patiently trying to pin his hump straight.

Several of the women were laughing uncontrollably. They had discovered that the capons were undercooked and, in consequence, virtually dagger-proof. One bird had skidded away from a slightly off-centre attack and its owner was now three tables distant, searching on hands and knees.

Richard III tried hard to think of a medieval insult to shout back to the quantity surveyor, but the general level of noise in the hall had been rising gradually until only the most raucous contributions now had any separate significance.

The band having launched into "Greensleeves Rock", Roy turned the amplifier up a notch. Richard III shrugged his hump and took a swig of sack. A bowl of bread hunks was slammed on the table. Here and there, a guest laid hold of his capon and made show of medieval voraciousness. Emboldened by example, others attacked their food. The stronger ones achieved actual dismemberment. Chicken legs were waved in triumph.

There was no doubt about it: the banquet was going well. Peter nodded in time with the pulsations of minstrelsy and allowed phrases of his preliminary report to assemble themselves in his mind. *Viability of low-profile catering situation geared up by broad-based euphoria elements* . . . He, too, was enjoying himself in his way.

Bernard, happy with his stopwatch, had moved from the Nellies' dressing-room to the kitchen. There, Arnold Hatch found him. There was some exchange of small talk. Then Hatch left to continue his tour of inspection.

At nine o'clock, Hatch was joined by Edmund Amis, who had been helping Margaret Shooter with some accounts relating to casual overnight accommodation in the motel extension. They ascended part of the staircase leading to the minstrels' gallery and looked together through a window that commanded a view of the Wassail Hall.

'Capacity house,' remarked Amis.

'Aye,' Hatch agreed, flatly.

There was a pause. Hatch's gaze moved slowly, systematically, across the scene below, like a mechanical scanner.

‘What they want, obviously,’ Amis said.

Hatch spotted Peter, decorously nibbling a chicken leg while he wrote something. A momentary feeling of doubt, of mistrust, Hatch dismissed irritably. Of course Eddie would pour cold water on anything like the Mackintosh-Brooke set-up. He’d feel his nose had been put out of joint.

‘One thing about those consultant blokes — they certainly put in some hours,’ Hatch said, a shade provocatively.

Amis seemed not to hear. He was chuckling. Hatch felt his arm nudged. ‘Look,’ said Amis. ‘Down there, in the first gangway.’

Hatch looked and understood.

‘It’s Joxy,’ he said. ‘Todd had to go off early tonight.’

Joxy attired in Todd’s jester outfit presented the appearance of a collapsed red and yellow tent with a frantic dwarf inside it. For a little while, Hatch and Amis watched its slow and erratic progress towards the top table. They saw, but could not hear, one of the Nellies deliver her prescribed oration: ‘Pray silence for the court jester, my lords and ladies.’ They did not wait to judge of Joxy’s effectiveness as a substitute target for the wit of the Baronial Board, but descended the stairs and made their way to Hatch’s office, where Julian still toiled blissfully and with a growing sense of wonder.

Chapter Sixteen

Inspector Purbright had gone home when a brief, but officially authenticated, biography of Mr Joseph Fortescue Tudor arrived by wire at Flaxborough police headquarters. A patrol car was dispatched at once to the inspector’s house, whence it brought him back to Fen Street.

From his office, he telephoned Sergeant Love's lodgings, the Floradora Club and the home of the chief constable, in that order and in rapid succession. The station duty sergeant meanwhile carried out his instruction to put two or three men on stand-by and to have transport instantly available.

Mr Chubb arrived in less than five minutes. Purbright received the impression that he was glad of an excuse to be out and about, but the chief constable was too loyal a dog breeder to admit that seven fractious Yorkshire terriers could be something of a trial at the day's end.

'No, no, Mr Purbright — not at all,' he declared in response to the inspector's apologies. 'Your call was fortuitous. This is Mrs Chubb's combing night.'

Purbright stared at him for a second, then, recovering himself, picked up the message that had been forwarded by London and handed it to Mr Chubb.

After reading a few lines, the chief constable raised his eyes. 'This is the fellow who arrived here the other day? Staying at the Roebuck.'

'Yes, sir.'

'Hmm.' Mr Chubb's eyes returned to the telegram. He read it through to the end slowly, then handed it back to Purbright.

'Incredible,' said Mr Chubb, gravely.

Purbright had been pondering. 'He must be a fair age,' he said. 'Capone went out of circulation in the very early 'thirties. So this Turidu can scarcely be less than sixty-five now.'

'Giuseppe Fortunino Turidu. . .' Mr Chubb recited the names carefully and with patent disapproval.

There was a knock. Love entered.

'Ah, sergeant. . .' Purbright always observed formalities in the presence of the chief constable.

'Sir?' So did Love.

'The man whom Detective Constable Burke is following has been identified. He is a criminal of considerable standing in the United States. A former lieutenant of Alphonse Capone, no less.'

Love looked impressed, but not alarmed; as might a tourist, shown a Roman catapult.

'His name,' Purbright went on, 'is Joe Turidu. In the old Chicago days, he was known by his intimates as The Tuner — a comical reference, apparently, to a certain dexterity with piano wire that he had cultivated. Neither at that time nor since has Mr Turidu been convicted on any criminal charge.'

'Extraordinary people, the Americans,' Mr Chubb interjected, shaking his head. 'That constitution of theirs was never properly thought out, you know. All sorts of scamps can take advantage of it.'

Purbright looked at his watch. 'I don't know what time that affair at Hatch's club winds up — the girl on his switchboard thought about half-past ten or eleven — but obviously Burke will need some backing before then. He must be sticking pretty closely to Tudor: he hasn't telephoned in yet.'

'We have no choice but to arrest this character, of course,' said Mr Chubb. 'Our own people must be protected. But is it enough simply to label him undesirable? One has to be so careful with foreigners nowadays.'

'He *is* the head of a criminal organisation,' Purbright observed. 'I'm sure the Home Office would back you up, sir.'

The chief constable looked doubtful.

Love, who had passed the time since his arrival by surreptitiously transcribing Mr Turidu's upside-down record, offered a suggestion.

'You could do him for passport misrepresentation, sir. He was born in Syracuse, Sicily. Burke says that it's Syracuse, New York, on his passport.'

Mr Chubb's brows rose with relief. 'That is most astute of you, sergeant. Thank you.' He turned to the inspector.

'I think I'll go along to my club for an hour now, Mr Purbright, if you think you can manage.'

By the time that Mr Padstowe's car had drawn close enough to the fugitive taxi for the silhouette of Tudor's head (or his hat, at least) to be discernible, the two vehicles were entering Flaxborough town centre. Burke instructed Padstowe to maintain distance until the taxi stopped.

But the taxi did not stop. After going down Fen Street, past the police station, it turned right into East Street, crossed the Market Place and made another right turn over the bridge into Northgate.

Within ten minutes, the houses thinned out into occasional bungalows and farm buildings. They were in the country. Steadily the taxi rolled on through the twilight.

Mr Padstowe, whose enthusiasm for the chase declined as his hunger increased, wanted to know if he should overtake in order that Burke might command the cab driver to halt in the name of the law; but Burke, rendered solemnly uncommunicative by a secret fear that he had ballsed something up, shook his head.

And so the procession of two continued on its way, along the road that led through Gosby and Hambourne to Chalmsbury and thence to the coastal resort of Brocklestone-upon-Sea.

Near Strawbridge, it passed a pair of vehicles bound for Flaxborough, bound, in fact, for the Floradora: a bus followed closely by a car.

In the car was Councillor Crispin, from the yard of whose splendid Brocklestone hotel, The Neptune, the expedition had set out.

In the bus sat three dozen men.

Because the interior lights of the bus were not switched on, neither Constable Burke nor anyone else on the road was likely to notice that the men were dressed in beast-skins and nursed in their hairy laps an assortment of helmets — somewhat in the manner of a planeful of paratroopers, save that these helmets were horned.

All the bus passengers were bearded, some by nature, the others by the same theatrical agency that had supplied, on Councillor Crispin's requisition 'for a charity concert', the skins and headgear.

On the luggage racks had been stowed clubs and swords. Shields, much more flimsy than they looked, were propped like briefcases, under seats.

The party was in high, but not riotous, spirits. If most of the members showed signs of a preliminary liquoring-up, it was clear also that they would have undergone such preparation with a full sense of professional responsibility. They remembered, and approved, Crispin's assertion that 'I wouldn't pick just any old bums for this job.'

Festivities at the banquet were beginning to flag a fraction. The capons had been disposed of by various means, as had the bread, and the sack ration was finished. Bowls of a sweet substance described in the prospectus as "possets and syllabubs" had been distributed and diagnosed by the critical as nothing more exotic than Sucro-wip's Insta-Creme. Other malcontents were taking advantage of the minstrels' refreshment interval to broadcast complaints that they had expected roast swan and a boar's head or two, not a cafeteria snack.

The less fastidious majority, though, was happy enough, if slightly restive. It was felt that some new impetus to the proceedings was needed. Even the first-class customers at the Baronial Board (who had been joined, a little late, by Mr Tudor in a Cardinal Wolsey set) seemed to be running low on jocosity. Some of the ladies had thankfully taken off their wimples.

The jester was perhaps the biggest disappointment of the evening. He was morose and hostile and had only one rejoinder to witty sallies — a gutteral expletive that sounded vaguely Russian. 'He's not as good as the fat one they had last week,' explained the quantity surveyor's wife defensively to her neighbour. 'I suppose they have to take what they can get these days.'

'Okfukov!' muttered the jester yet again.

In the minstrels' gallery, Roy and his Rockadours were getting back into harness and adjusting microphones. The Nellies, plying to and from the bar with trays of tankards, patiently explained rules. 'It's not beer, it's ale, see? And if you call "Miss" I won't serve you — you've got to shout out "Ho Wench!" Right?' One of the electronic lutes gave forth a sample note like a chimney stack falling through a corrugated iron roof. Maid Marion looked aloft and waved cheerily to her husband.

Suddenly her movements froze. Her smile faded and became a stare of incredulity.

Roy, still clutching his lute, was being lifted above the head of a whiskered giant clad in what looked like a hearth rug. Thongs of hide criss-crossed the giant's legs, which were thick and knotted like blackthorn trunks. On his head and jammed low over wild, red-rimmed eyes, was a helmet flanked by cow horns.

The giant bellowed. The whole assembly turned and stared upward. Maid Marion, convinced that her husband was about to be hurled out of the minstrels' gallery, screeched. Other people applauded. They assumed the act to be part of the entertainment.

When Roy was lowered, not precipitately into the hall, but more gently if not much less spectacularly into the Rockadours' drum kit, the plaudits doubled.

'Oh, yes,' explained Mrs Goshawk to the members of the Hambourne Women's Institute, this sort of thing often happened in the Middle Ages. Vikings, you know.'

The ladies murmured appreciation.

'Very cleverly got up,' said Mrs Goshawk.

There was a dreadful yell a few feet behind her. She and her companions jumped in unison, then turned in time to see another hairy athlete leap upon the next table and begin to swing a double-edged axe around.

'It's to symbolise our being put to the sword,' Mrs Goshawk confided to those nearest to her. One or two clutched their handbags and pushed back their seats a little.

From the body of the hall rose more clapping and some shouts of encouragement for the unscheduled diversion.

Three more Vikings appeared near the kitchen entrance. They advanced, whooping and growling.

'Norse,' explained Mrs Goshawk. She added: 'Of course, in the real thing, they would have been deflowering everybody.'

Sounds of high commotion in the kitchen were succeeded by the bursting upon the scene of a whole platoon of Vikings. Some were pushing liquor trolleys piled with bottles of all kinds. These they proceeded to distribute with ferocious bonhomie amongst the guests, who, once they had recovered from their natural astonishment, broached and set about sinking the gifts before they could be snatched away again.

Back and forth rumbled the trolleys, bringing fresh relays of port and sherry and whisky, madeira and gin and burgundy, clarets and sauternes, rum and moselles and brandy, kirsch and Benedictine and Calvados.

At first, the Nellies loyally voiced objection to the traffic and tried to remonstrate with the raiders, but they were soon rounded up and herded into a storeroom where diligent administration of port and compliments rapidly rendered them tractable and even affectionate.

The antics of the men in skins and helmets were enjoyed enormously by the party from the Chalmsbury Darby and Joan Club. 'It's a history pageant, you see,' one of the more confident members explained as he prised the seal off a bottle of Grand Marnier with his thumb nail. 'Them's Roundheads.' He poured and immediately swigged a half tumbler. 'Here, Maggie, have some orange squash, girl.' Maggie shook her back-tilted head disdainfully; she was enjoying for the first time in a long life the sensation of drinking crème de menthe straight from the neck.

Within twenty minutes of the raiders' first appearance, half the guests were glassily, irremediably drunk. The reckless intake of exotic and highly alcoholic liquors in bizarre combination exerted upon unseasoned drinkers a powerfully anaesthetic effect. Some simply slumped across the table as if they had been shot in the back of the head. Others fell off their chairs, truffled around a while, then curled in snoring sleep. A wilful minority remained sitting upright, talking incoherently but earnestly to no one in particular until consciousness ebbed to leave them, wide-eyed and waxy, like preserved victims of some sudden Vesuvian disaster.

Among the half who did not pass out — a curious coalition of near-abstainers and hardened topers — there was a wide variety of behaviour. A number of nervous and outraged guests tried to leave the hall, but they were rudely repulsed from the exits by Vikings on guard duty. They had to be content with sitting around and grumbling to one another about the organisers having gone too far and this sort of thing being not what they had expected and wasn't it time that something was done about orgies because that's what this was and no mistake.

The disgruntled had a point. To the accompaniment of a Viking trio making sounds upon the Rockadours' captured instruments like a prolonged railway accident, the merriest element among the still conscious guests was set on a mixed programme of destruction, exhibitionism and, where opportunity offered, fornication. In this last matter, valuable assistance was forthcoming from some of the Nellies, port-primed and paroled from their storeroom gaol for the purpose.

Peter, sober still and dedicated to the higher aims of

Mackintosh-Brooke, sat on amidst the chaos and made notes while light lasted.

This was not to be for much longer. What had started as an aimless throwing around of platters and tankards and bottles (Peter's *selection by client freewill of optimum enjoyment posture*) was developing, with Viking encouragement, into systematic bombardment of every lamp in the place. One by one, the simulated flambeaux were quenched by a bursting bottle or lopped by a skilfully spun platter. Tankards soared to the rafters, made execution among the electric bulbs and fell out of the resulting gloom upon heads rendered indifferent and strangely wound–proof by prodigious quantities of alcohol.

By the time that only one lamp remained alight in a comparatively inaccessible corner of the roof, even the most disapproving watched with fascination the flight of the missiles. Eventually, a lucky ricochet sent a wildly directed platter straight to the target. The pop of the implosion and the drench of dark that it brought were acknowledged with a great tipsy cheer. For a moment after there was silence. Then came sounds of scuffling and heaving penetrated by squeals. But nothing more was thrown.

A slit of brilliant light expanded to a broad rectangle. Big black shapes, bushy and horned, moved across it.

'They're going,' whispered Mrs Goshawk to those members of the Hambourne Women's Institute who had spurned the gift of strong waters and consequently were still capable of being instructed. 'Back to the long ships, you know. Mind you, if it had been the real thing they'd have taken us as well.' She shuddered deliciously.

The raiders indeed were leaving. They mustered quickly and quietly in the kitchen, checked their armament, then filed into the corridor and out of the nearest door. A few minutes later, a bus left the parking area behind the club. It was followed immediately by a car.

Somebody found the door and fastened it open. It admitted enough light for survivors to pick their way through the ruins of the feast and escape into the kitchen.

They heard muffled shouts. Fists pounded against the inside of the door of the Tiring Roome of Ye Serving Wenches. When it was unlocked, there emerged three non-collaborating Nellies, the four missing members of the kitchen staff, one business efficiency consultant, and a very angry Wassail Master.

'Whose idea,' demanded Mr Hubbard of his rescuers, 'was it to let those sods loose? Bloody jesters and troobadoors and all that's one thing, but I'm not having my staff molested by a lot of dressed up bloody apes. Where's Hatch? I tell you I'm not putting up with it.'

And he steamed off along the corridor.

The Nellies peered into the dimness of the banqueting hall. 'Christ!' said one, fervently.

Bernard took a look over their shoulders. He had not lost his habitual expression of amiable, alert curiosity, but there was something about the way he subsequently checked his stopwatch against the pressure gauge on the main oven that suggested some degree of temporary disorientation.

Edmund Amis entered.

'Anyone seen Mr Hatch? Mr Hubbard's rushing round in circles looking for him.'

Shrugs and blank stares.

'Well, he's certainly not in the gaming room. And he wouldn't have gone home without saying anything to me.'

Amis glanced at a few faces, then fixed on Bernard as seemingly the least confused person present. 'What's been going on, anyway?'

'My reading, quite frankly,' said Bernard, 'is that there have been a number of counterproductive developments, but I have no specific recall of events in this regard.'

A junior cook found voice. 'A lot of fellows dressed in skins and that. They locked us up. And some of the girls too. And then they sort of took over the banquet. That's what Heather said.' He indicated an angular, worried-looking girl whose person was much more modestly accommodated in her orange-seller's costume than appeared to be the general rule.

Heather nodded. 'And they got in the wine and spirit store and gave away the whole lot. Just *gave* it away. Handed it out.' Her voice was husky with horror.

More people were coming through from the stricken hall. 'Can we get to the buses this way?' timidly inquired a pair of old ladies. One wore no shoes; the other carried an unopened bottle of cherry brandy, holding it before her by its neck as if lighting herself to bed.

Amis beckoned the junior cook and one of the kitchen hands. 'Go and help look for Mr Hatch,' he told them. 'Try his office and anywhere else you can think of. See if Mrs Shooter knows where he is, but don't go into the motel area without asking her first.'

There was a distant clang. The members of the band had repossessed themselves of their instruments and were now testing them for damage by the light of an auxiliary lamp in the minstrels' gallery that had not been switched on during the bombardment.

Amis surveyed the scene in the Wassail Hall, which even the conscientious Peter had deserted at last (to seek out his two colleagues for an over-all debriefing in regard to that particular point in time). Then he called lounge, gaming-room and bar on the house telephone. Every member of staff who could possibly be spared, he said, should come to the club kitchen at once. It was an emergency. Mr Hatch, when he arrived, would undoubtedly confirm this request.

Amis had just completed his third call when Hubbard, grey-faced and shaping soundless words with lips the colour of dead violets, stepped falteringly through the doorway. The young cook was beside him. He looked terrified and sick, but held Hubbard's arm in what support he could give.

Hubbard groped for a chair. Someone pulled it round to receive him. He sank heavily down, his head bowed. A glass was held before him, but he seemed not to see it, not to see anything. 'Oh, Christ!' he said. Then again, 'Oh, Christ!'

They waited, listening to him breathe. The cook, appealed to by glances, just shook his head and stood leaning against a table, silent.

Hubbard roused himself at last. He raised his eyes slowly and looked from one to another, as upon strangers in a crowd. His lips had begun to move again.

'He's dead. The poor old sod's dead. Somebody's blown half his bloody head off.'

Chapter Seventeen

Purbright and Love and a levy of five other policemen entered the Floradora Club within less than ten minutes of Hubbard's discovery of his slain employer, but the news of the death had already invested the place with silence and bewilderment. No one made any attempt to leave. Roulette, chemmy and blackjack ceased as promptly and with as little argument as if they had suddenly become work. Both bars were left untended, but no one seemed inclined to commit the irreverence of helping himself. Only the banqueting hall remained isolated from the sobering chemistry of shock. Its occupants, strewn in disorder, were either utterly insensible or else grappled and grunted in semi-comatose bliss with partners half flesh and half dream.

Inspector Purbright surveyed the scene.

'Looks like Belshazzar's Feast.'

Two constables were detailed to get some lights

restored and to take an inventory, as far as proved possible, of those present.

Detective Burke, returned in deep disgrace after his chase of Joseph Tudor's hat, was instructed very sharply to conduct a personal and unremitting search for Giuseppe Turidu and to detain him for questioning. He set off with a torch lent him by a more provident colleague and began working his way along the rows of tables in the banqueting hall like a stretcher bearer checking for survivors after a battle.

A fourth policeman was set to guard the entrance to the corridor which led to Hatch's office and sitting-room and to the small washroom in which Hatch had been found.

The inspector gave the body a cursory examination from the doorway. There was a lot of blood about. He took care not to tread in any. The police surgeon and the squad from the forensic science laboratory would be properly equipped for closer dealings.

The washroom door bore no sign of damage round the lock; presumably it had been ajar or simply latched when Hubbard had come in search of his employer. In the upper part of the door, at about the level of Purbright's head, was a roughly crescent-shaped area of perforation and splintering. Most of the glass had been smashed out of the small square window opposite the door. The inspector saw several whitish fragments on the floor. A thin, cold breeze flowed past him. Its freshness only emphasised the steamy, overheated air of the cubicle, smelling of soap and hot towelling and now charged with the sickly-sweet scent of blood.

Purbright pointed to the window and touched Love's sleeve. 'Go round the outside, Sid, and see what you can find before anybody gets trampling around. I'm going to set up shop in the office next door.'

Love hurried off. A few moments later his careful step could be heard on gravel. An unpromising material,

Purbright well knew, but had there ever *really* existed a murderer so considerate as to prance around on a flower bed?

Before he left, he looked down once more on the sprawled body of Hatch, jacketless, one shirt sleeve rolled up. The cuff of the other, unbuttoned, sodden with darkening blood, was plastered flat to the floor. A comb lay in one corner. The wash basin was still half full of water, rimmed with grey soap scum. The water depths were pink, the white porcelain of the basin slashed with scarlet rain. As Purbright saw these things, he felt the pity and the anger that murder unfailingly stirred in him. The waste, the indignity, the loneliness of such a death — these were appalling enough, whoever and whatever the victim, but that they had been exacted coldly and ruthlessly in pursuance of profit (and here, Purbright told himself, was a money crime if ever he saw one) utterly defied rationality.

With the arrival of a pair of patrol cars, in one of which Mrs Hatch had been brought from Primrose Mount, Purbright's forces of occupation were increased by four. More methodical deployment was not possible.

The inspector gave instructions for all guests and customers to be assembled in the gaming-room, where he would talk to them briefly. They would then be allowed to go home after their names and addresses had been recorded. There was no point, said Purbright, in trying to intern a crowd of tired and resentful people.

Members of the club staff, though, would have to be prepared for a slightly longer stay so that he and Sergeant Love might question them personally and in turn. They could make themselves comfortable in the lounge.

Two patrolmen were sent to make a round of the motel chalets and ensure that none contained a guest, whether officially or unofficially. Purbright gave the order flatly, as if on an afterthought. It would not do, he reflected, to betray to conventionally-minded policemen his tenuous private hope that they would stumble upon one or two of those elusive nuns, profanely transformed. *Nunnae in flagrante delicto.*

When Love re-entered the office he was carrying a shot-gun by the handkerchief-enwrapped end of its barrel.

'Propped against the wall outside,' he explained.

Purbright peered at the gun, detail by detail, without touching it. 'Very nice,' he murmured at last. 'A choice fowling piece. Not the murderer's of course. He wouldn't have ditched a thousand quid's worth of gun.'

Love puffed his shiny, schoolboyish cheeks. 'Crikey!'

'It's probably his own. Hatch's. His wife should know.' Purbright spread sheets of typing paper on a table. The sergeant carefully lowered the shot-gun to rest upon them, its barrel pointing away into a corner.

'I'll see her first, Sid, then Fairclough can drive her back home. Tell him to find a neighbour to stay with her.'

When Love had left, Purbright put more sheets of paper on the gun, nearly covering it.

A knock on the door; an inthrust head, perkily solicitous.

'Now, then, squire, where's the doings?'

Purbright recognised from tone rather than features the man he had last seen toting test tubes twelve years before. The Hopjoy case. And here he was, still eager-beavering. Incredible.

'How nice to see you again, Mr. . .' He rose, trying to disguise in movement his having forgotten the name.

'Warlock.' The man dealt Purbright a vigorous handshake, then punched the palm of his own left hand several times, as though trying out a new knuckleduster. He simultaneously did a little side-skipping dance.

'Of course. How are you?'

'Great, squire.' Mr Warlock (a sergeant still? — surely not) lowered his chin and tucked it into his left shoulder.

'Absolutely great.' He made one or two jabs into nothing with his fist. 'So where is it, then?'

Purbright was aware suddenly that Warlock was accompanied; he glimpsed boots and blue raincoats and a bundle of polythene sheeting over somebody's arm.

'Along here.' He led the way. 'You won't all be able to get in at once. Incidentally' — he dropped his voice — 'I'd be glad if you'd keep the place closed as much as possible. His wife will be coming by this way in a few moments.'

And soon the widow did come by, escorted by Love, who paused to shield her from the sight of the shut and shattered door. Purbright had asked that someone in the kitchen should maintain supplies of tea and coffee. He gave Mrs Hatch a cup from the tray on the desk.

She seemed fragile, timorous, oddly shrunken. But there were no tears.

'A number of things have been going on here tonight, Mrs Hatch, and I haven't been able to obtain any explanation. Perhaps you can help me understand.'

She made a faint movement of assent, then stared absently at the carpet. The fingers of one hand fiddled with pleats of dress material near her throat. The meticulous manicure of latter years had failed to disguise housework's legacy of wrinkles and enlarged knuckles.

'I'm told, for instance,' said Purbright, 'that the banquet did not follow the usual course — that events got out of hand, in fact. Can you tell me if your husband knew what was going to happen — or what was *supposed* to happen, I should say, because I don't imagine a near riot was what he intended.'

'Oh, no; I'm sure he didn't.'

'Dressing up, charades, fanciful entertainments of that kind — these were features of the banquets, I believe.'

'Certainly. They are very popular. But always in good taste. Arnie would never . . .' The restless fingers stole to chin, to mouth.

The inspector waited a moment.

Mrs Hatch looked up. 'Eddie — Mr Amis — told me just now that there had been some sort of a raid by people from outside the club. It was very nasty behaviour, he said. Mr Amis is my husband's private secretary.'

'And he'd seen this affair — this raid — going on, had he?'

'No, no. Mr Hubbard told him about it. Mr Hubbard is staff. He and Mr Amis were discussing it with the young men from my husband's business consultancy.'

Purbright tilted his head a little to one side. 'Who are they, Mrs Hatch?'

'I'm afraid I don't know their names except as Peter and Bernard and Julian. They are not employees, you understand, but consultants. Very well spoken, although their firm is American, I believe.'

Mrs Hatch was not too shocked or grieved to be trying hard to be well spoken herself, Purbright noticed. One of his dissatisfactions with his calling was the way it seemed to bring out either the worst in people or what they regrettably imagined to be the best.

'Had Mr Hatch any interests, any business interests, in America, do you know?'

She shook her head. 'Oh, no, nothing like that.'

'Was he . .' Purbright paused, aware of the need to frame this question very carefully. 'Did he ever give employment to people from abroad? Through some religious organisation, perhaps? I am thinking of young women, for instance, who might have been glad of work in a club in this country to help them learn the language.'

Mrs Hatch reacted to this probe with a stare of such patent incomprehension that Purbright immediately waved the subject aside. Even if Mrs Hatch had been privy to some or most of her husband's dealings, he was scarcely likely to have entrusted her with knowledge of so exotic an enterprise as nun-napping.

'I have to tell you,' he went on, gently, 'that your

husband was killed with a shot gun. He must have died immediately, perhaps quite unaware of what had happened. I have that gun here. I want you to look at it and tell me if you think you have seen it before.'

He drew aside the sheets of typing paper.

Mrs Hatch glanced at the gun and turned away at once. She nodded miserably.

'It's Arnie's.'

'You are sure?'

'Oh, quite sure. He bought it last year to go shooting. It's a very good gun; he had to go to London for it.'

'And he used it last season, did he?'

She hesitated. 'Well, not actually, no. He rented what they call a shoot — a bit of land, really — but it wasn't suitable.'

Purbright fought down a mad impulse to add 'Not shootable, in fact,' and asked instead where Hatch had kept his gun. She said she had last noticed it in her husband's private sitting-room along the corridor.

'Mrs Hatch, did you know that your husband had received a letter threatening his life?'

She stared. 'I most certainly did not. Who would do a thing like that?'

'We don't know, but the letter came from America.'

'America?' Her puzzlement was absolute. The inspector retreated from that dead end.

'Just one more question for now, Mrs Hatch. Forget the letter — just tell me if you know of anyone, anyone at all, whom your husband might have considered an enemy.'

Her shoulders stiffened, tendons jerked into prominence amidst the flaccid flesh of the neck, her mouth set in prim dislike.

'Tonight, inspector (genteel indignation raised the merest ghost of an aspirate before the word) 'more than £370 worth of very high quality liquid refreshments were stolen from the club stockroom and handed out to all and sundry by a gang of hooligans. If that isn't the work of an enemy, I don't know what is.'

Purbright, marvelling at the promptness and precision of the widow's stocktaking, asked if she had any idea who was responsible.

'Oh, certainly,' she replied. 'The same *gentleman*' (bitter emphasis here) 'who's been waging a vendetta and that's what it is, a vendetta — against me and poor Arnie for a long time. He's behind it, all right. *Councillor* — so called — *Councillor* Harry Crispin. And *her* as well, of course, but that goes without saying.'

'Mrs Crispin?'

'*Missus* Crispin! Ho, ho, ho.' Mrs Hatch's acidulated mirth would have etched glass.

Before conducting any more personal interviews, Purbright set about the release of the hundred or so customers and guests penned in the gaming-room. All had identified themselves, some very reluctantly, and the crowd now displayed an aggrieved restiveness more appropriate to transit camps than to country clubs.

The inspector stated baldly what had happened. He asked if anyone had heard a noise that could have been the firing of a gun, a shotgun: as dwellers in a country area, most of them would know what that sounded like.

The question brought no response at all. It was clear, Purbright reflected, that the washroom, with its closed door and its single tiny window, through which the gun had been thrust before firing, must have acted as a kind of silencer.

Had Mr Hatch been seen that evening by anyone present? A murmur of assent. Where? Bar — gaming-room — lounge — it was his usual tour of the place, they supposed: keeping an eye on things. Time? Oh, half-past nine, perhaps ten; no one had especially noticed.

Did anyone recall seeing a rather dark-complexioned man, heavily-built, not tall, in his sixties but alert-looking, probably with an American accent? Silence. A few head shakes.

'Thank you, ladies and gentlemen. I'm sorry you've been kept waiting about. If anything occurs to any of you later, don't hesitate to get in touch with me.'

They filed out, suddenly voluble, as though from an exciting film.

Sergeant Love had begun taking statements from members of the staff. He was by nature friendly, eager to please, and in consequence easily sidetracked. Thus, although he learned little or nothing relevant to the murder of their employer, he was treated by the interviewees to glimpses of life behind the bar, the roulette wheel and the serving counter which, he afterwards confessed to the inspector, had gee-whizzed him no little. Part of his sense of wonder had been engendered (though this he did not admit) by the revelatory nature of the costumes of the girls, who quite unselfconsciously presented themselves for questioning in their working gear.

It was as well, perhaps, that the susceptible sergeant did not share the discoveries of Patrolmen Brevitt and Heaney in their search of the motel chalets.

Despite strong objections by Mrs Shooter, whom they left gesticulating and threatening in her boudoir, Brevitt and Heaney set off stolidly in opposite circuits. By the time they met, half way round, they had trawled seven hastily dressed gentlemen and four club hostesses, whose claim to have been simply 'turning down the beds' on the manageress's instructions seemed to the policemen almost as laughable a subterfuge as the assertion by a trio of young gentlemen that they were engaged in a time and motion study.

Chapter Eighteen

The Chief Constable quietly entered the office in which Purbright was finishing the last interview he thought it reasonable to get through that night. It was with one of the girls Brevitt and Heaney had escorted from the chalets.

Mr Chubb stood close against the side wall and watched in silence. He looked like a schools inspector, observing a lesson.

The girl had been explaining to Purbright that although her real name was Janice Wilkinson, she was known in the club by both staff and customers as Daisy. It was a rule that every hostess had to have a flower name. Mr Hatch liked flower names because they gave the club a nicer tone . . . Oh, dear, but was it true about poor Mr . . . Yes, the inspector said, it was quite true, unfortunately.

'How old are you, Janice?'

'Daisy,' she corrected. 'I'm nineteen.'

'You like club work, do you?'

'Oh, yes. It's super. I want to be a Bunny, though. In a Bunny Club.'

The chief constable stared at her as if she had just expressed a literal zoological ambition.

'Where is your home, Daisy?' Purbright asked.

'My mum and dad live in Chalmsbury. I'm in digs here with one of the other girls.'

'But Mrs Shooter lets you stay in one of the chalets occasionally, does she?'

'When I've been working late.'

'And the other girls?'

'Them too. Now and then. Well, it's a long way out, isn't it?'

'And of course the motel isn't needed yet, because it isn't properly finished. Right?'

Daisy nodded cheerfully. 'That's right. Yes.' She rewarded the inspector's friendly percipience by shifting in her chair so as to redeploy her parts to their greater advantage.

Mr Chubb stared with grave preoccupation at a wall calendar opposite and began to tap his pursed lips with the knuckle of his right forefinger.

'How did you come to take this job, Daisy?' Purbright went on.

'A friend of mine worked here and I wanted to do modelling in those days and this friend said she sometimes did modelling here so I came along and asked Mr Hatch and he said yes I think I can use you.'

'And do you do modelling?'

A slight pause. 'Sort of.'

The answer seemed to satisfy the inspector. 'Now then,' he said, 'I want you to think carefully about all your other friends here — the Flowers, they're called — is that right? (She nodded and made a face.) Yes, well I want you to tell me if any of these girls are from other countries.'

'What, *foreigners*, you mean?' Her expression plainly refuted so unwholesome a notion.

'They are all English, are they? You're sure?'

'Course I'm sure. Except Heather's from somewhere up in Scotland. And Rose is Birmingham. Mostly they're from round here.'

Very diffidently, Purbright put his final question.

'I suppose none of them has made mention at any time of having been in a convent?'

Janice/Daisy suspended for a moment an effort to make her left breast more comfortable by probing around inside her brassiere with two fingers of the opposite hand.

'A *what*?'

'A convent. A nunnery.'

She squirmed, frowning; then withdrew the hand, examined it, and flicked away a retrieved cracker crumb.

'I shouldn't think so. I mean, what would they be doing in a place like that?'

When the girl had gone — dismissed with a degree of respectful courtesy that left her wondering if she should not go a-hostessing in aeroplanes instead of clubs — the chief constable told Purbright that he feared there was a side to the late Mr Hatch that was far from creditable.

Purbright unblushingly said that he was coming round to Mr Chubb's view.

'A dreadful end, though, Mr Purbright, just the same. What a savage thing to do.'

'Savage, indeed, sir. Or desperate.'

Chubb made no comment but he had marked the alternative. He raised his brow.

'Taking a shotgun to a man,' said the inspector, 'is an especially violent and brutal act. I have been trying to think of all the situations in which it might be considered characteristic. There really are very few.'

'It cannot be justified in any situation.'

'No, sir, but I am talking about likelihood, not justification. For instance, the use of a shotgun in a robbery involving a great deal of money no longer surprises us, however reprehensible we consider it.'

Mr Chubb conceded the point with regret.

'One hears of shotgun weddings,' continued Purbright, 'but there are shotgun divorces, too. That appalling blast would be peculiarly appropriate to a crime of passion or vengefulness.

'It is also a weapon of terror, sir. That is why it is so much favoured by gangsters on the one hand and by those of strong religious convictions on the other.'

'I do not think,' said the chief constable, in the very centre of whose smooth, churchwarden's cheek a tiny flush had suddenly appeared, 'that you need go any further with these speculations, Mr Purbright. As you somewhat superfluously point out, the shotgun is traditionally associated with gangsters. A known gangster was in this place tonight. His associates had earlier given warning of an intended crime. You know your own business best, no doubt, but I must say I expected to see more obvious effort being made to trace this man before he can do any more damage.'

The inspector looked not repentant, but bewildered.

'I'm sorry, sir. I hadn't realised that you thought Tudor was responsible for the shooting.'

'Well, damn it all, of course I do. What else did you expect?'

The revealing forthrightness of this response was instantly regretted by Mr Chubb, but Purbright's store of magnanimity had not been entirely exhausted by a night of boring interviews. He smiled broadly, as if to acknowledge a shaft of cunning irony.

'You are perfectly right,' he said, 'to challenge my perhaps too ready acceptance of Tudor's innocence. Now then, sir — reasons . . .' He placed fingertips together and for a moment, lightly touched his chin in a contemplative gesture.

'This Tudor, or Turidu, is undeniably a very wicked fellow, as you say, sir. In the days of Prohibition, he was a professional murderer — so professional, indeed, that he succeeded in avoiding indictment, let alone conviction, during the whole of the bootlegging era. He has no record, only a history. And the fact that it is tinged with mythology — he is believed, for instance, to have had a hand in the St Valentine's Day massacre in Chicago — is testimony to the high regard in which Mr Tudor is held in his own country.

'However, he no longer is a criminal in an executive sense, having moved, like so many of his successful colleagues, into the fields of administration and patronage. Our information is that Mr Tudor's political influence is considerable, though not overt. He is listed, for example, as one of the vice-presidents of the Nixonian Institute of Public Welfare.

'You may well be wondering' (Mr Chubb most certainly was) 'what such a man is doing here at all. We shall have the opportunity of asking him in person before much longer. I had word half an hour ago that the officer who had been keeping him under observation was waiting for him to regain consciousness.'

Sudden alarm showed in the chief constable's face. 'I trust there's no question of force hav. . .'

'No, no, sir,' Purbright interrupted. 'The man's simply asleep, that's all. Quite a number of the people in the big dining-hall over there were being encouraged to drink rather injudiciously earlier in the evening. I shall tell you about that in a moment. The submission I wanted to make, though, is that no one in Tudor's position, with all his achievements and advantages, is going to be so mad as to come all this way and risk exchanging Miami or San Clemente, or wherever these people live their good life, for our Lincoln Gaol.'

For a long while, the chief constable pondered. At intervals over the past twenty years or so, he had been visited with a fleeting but alarming fantasy. It took the form of an impression that crime (which was a simple equation of sin in Mr Chubb's philosophy) was being smuggled over those social borders that once had effectively contained it, and was being taken up and cultivated as a sort of fashionable demonic hobby by a whole range of highly respectable persons, his own erstwhile peers and superiors. At such moments of terrible suspicion, it would not have surprised him overmuch to learn that a lord lieutenant had burgled a neighbouring manor house, nor that a Conservative Member of Parliament had turned tax swindler.

And now, at last, it was beginning to occur to Mr Chubb's mind that his lapses into apostasy, however brief and infrequent, were invariably shadowed by the lanky, benign, gentle-mannered figure of Purbright. A good policeman, not a doubt of it. But he possessed what

Mr Chubb would have called 'odd streaks' in his nature. No ambition. A reluctance to accept and apply straightforward moral rules. A strange deficiency of indignation. And always that scepticism . . . What was the use of a man showing humility if he never for a moment surrendered the sovereignty of his opinions?

'Very well, then,' said the chief constable, in a no-nonsense tone that signified a sudden determination to be Svengalied, so to speak, no longer by his inspector, 'if this Sicilian fellow didn't shoot Hatch, perhaps you can tell me who did.'

'No, sir.'

'Ah.' Mr Chubb looked satisfied and challenging at the same time.

'Mrs Hatch,' said Purbright, carelessly, 'says that Councillor Henry Crispin shot her husband.'

'Good grief!'

The inspector waited a moment.

'There has been a good deal of acrimony between them for some time, sir,' he went on. 'Almost a feud, in fact.'

'Yes, but murder . . .'

'Oh, I agree, sir. I fancy Mrs Hatch was overwrought. It would be understandable in the circumstances.'

There was a knock at the door. Sergeant Love entered.

'We've arrested a bloke who was trying to hide in a cupboard along the corridor there, sir,' said Love to Purbright. 'He'd got an axe with him, but he wasn't violent or anything.'

'I see.' There was in Purbright's voice a rise that invited elucidation.

'He's got nothing on except boots and a kind of dog's skin thing.' Blandly, the sergeant added: 'He says he missed his bus.'

'What could be more natural?' Purbright turned to Mr Chubb. 'This must be one of the raiding party we've been hearing about tonight. The object seems to have been to sabotage the banquet. Quite a deal of liquor was taken out of store and given away.'

Love had further information to offer. 'Brevitt says he's seen the bloke before. He's one of the attendants in that amusement park at Brocklestone.'

'Crispin's amusement park,' remarked Purbright in an aside to the chief constable.

'And some of the girls, the waitresses, say that they recognised fellows from the same place,' Love said. 'That's how they were so good at jumping around from table to table, the girls said — they were from the dodgem cars.'

'All right, sergeant. You'd better take a statement from this man. We particularly want to know who recruited him and gave the instructions. If he's forthcoming don't bother to charge him with anything; we can do without complications of that kind at the moment.'

Not long after the sergeant's departure, there was another knock on the door, a timid double tap. Purbright called 'Come in' but without effect. A few moments later, the knock was repeated. The inspector rose and opened the door himself.

Standing outside was the chastened Detective Constable Burke. It was not he who caught Purbright's eye, however, but a figure in scarlet robe and hat — the presentment (a trifle grubby and rumpled, but splendid still) of one who had suffered an even more notable fall from grace.

Burke stiffly introduced Cardinal Wolsey's reincarnation.

'Joseph Tudor, sir. Alias Turidu.'

Purbright motioned Tudor inside. Burke he dismissed not unkindly with instructions to see if Sergeant Love could find him something useful to do.

Beneath the red prelate's hat, two sleepy but wary eyes shifted in shadow as Tudor looked from Purbright to Chubb and back again. His jowls, swollen now with resentment and incipient hangover, were the shape and colour of aubergines. At even intervals, the nose flexed in a sharp, questing sniff.

Purbright announced his and Chubb's identities and asked to see Tudor's passport. Without a word Tudor groped amidst the folds of his too-long robe.

After examining the passport, Purbright said that there appeared to be some discrepancy between that document and the records of the United States immigration authorities. Would Mr Tudor care to say whether he was, as a matter of verifiable fact, an American or an Italian citizen?

Mr Tudor replied in a brusque, gravelly, not-well-pleased voice, which he seemed to produce as a special favour and on a very short lease. He was, he affirmed, a citizen of the United States and couldn't British cops read their own goddam language?

Mr Chubb said he thought there was no call for Mr Tudor — if such indeed was his name — to adopt that kind of tone.

Mr Tudor grunted and extended a hand to receive back the passport. The interview, he seemed to have decided, was over.

'I'm sorry, sir,' said the inspector, 'but I must ask you to bear with us for a while longer. The inquiries respecting your passport will be made with the least possible delay.'

There was a sound like a leaking steam valve. It was prolonged for several seconds before blooming into '*Santa Maria!*' — most devoutly delivered between clenched teeth.

'Yes, sir,' Purbright acknowledged. He went on: 'While you are here, I have a number of other questions I wish to put to you, Mr Tudor. And in fairness I ought to point out that these questions are part of the investigation we are making into the death a few hours ago of the owner of this club.'

Tudor, utterly sober now, balled a podgy fist and held it against his temple. His eyes were upturned in self-accusatory exasperation. Mr Chubb, noting with disapproval the drink-inflamed whites thus displayed, was impressed nevertheless with their owner's performance. A murderer, surely, would react to mention of his crime with pretence of shock or ignorance or even disbelief. He would not behave as though he had just remembered leaving a tap running.

'The guy got hit, then, huh?' Mr Tudor shook his head, but he looked more annoyed than regretful.

Purbright was watching him closely. 'He did, indeed.'

Again Mr Tudor gave his head a shake. He noisily sucked a bit of banquet out of a tooth and began to nibble it.

'Too bad,' he said.

'Why have you come to England?' Purbright asked, after waiting a while.

Mr Tudor shrugged. 'Maybe I go for this Middle Ages stuff.' He found another tooth to suck. 'And maybe I do some business here.' Again he shrugged. It was quite an accomplishment with him.

'The East Anglian olive crop?' inquired Purbright.

British sarcasm was not to Mr Tudor's taste. He gave the inspector a smile that looked as if a dentist had lifted his lip with a probe.

'I gather you do not wish to tell me the real reason for your presence in Flaxborough,' Purbright said.

Tudor did another lip lift, this time for Mr Chubb's benefit. 'He *gathers*, this guy.'

'Where are you staying, sir?' Purbright's tone was as pleasant as ever.

'This Roebuck Arms joint — your village inn, I guess.'

'An officer will drive you there, sir, so that you may collect what things you need before he takes you on.'

'On? On where?'

'To the village lock-up, sir, as one might say.'

Tudor's face darkened so rapidly and to such degree that the sight of it was like watching a great bruise develop. Mr Chubb took advantage of the man's deprivation of speech to emphasise, somewhat prosaically, the seriousness of passport irregularities in the view of the British Home Office.

'I want my lawyer,' growled Mr Tudor as soon as he was able. He banged the desk with his fist. 'And get my consul, but quick.'

The chief constable assured him that such matters would be attended to by the appropriate officer at police headquarters as soon as Mr Tudor took up temporary residence.

Purbright mentioned to Mr Chubb that American consular affairs, so far as Flaxborough was concerned, were in the hands of Mr Brisson, the shipping agent. 'He's the Italian consul as well, as a matter of fact,' he thought it right to add.

To Mr Tudor, the inspector said: 'I imagine your own attorney would understand if you sought advice from a local man on this occasion, would he not?'

The thumb that had slipped safety catches on behalf of the late Mr Capone, pulled piano wire into the truculent tracheae of half the henchmen of the late Mr O'Banion, and, in more recent, peaceable, years, counted off enough hundred-dollar bills into presidential campaign laundries to buy respectability for the duration of its owner's twilight years — this thumb now jerked in the direction of Inspector Purbright.

'He *imagines! Gathering* ain't enough, so now he *imagines!* He talks so pretty I could cry!'

When, divested of his cardinalship and in the close custody of a marvellously alert Detective Burke, Mr Tudor had departed, the chief constable gave Purbright a worried stare.

'And do you still mean to say, Mr Purbright, that you rule out that dreadful fellow as the murderer of poor Hatch?'

'Without hesitation, sir,' said the inspector, cheerfully.

Chapter Nineteen

Somewhat to the surprise of the duty sergeant, it was not a lawyer whom Mr Tudor required to be brought to his cell the following morning, but a lady.

The sergeant consulted Purbright, who was intrigued. Yes, he said, let him see the lady in question — if she would come, of course; that was up to her.

'But this Miss Teatime, sir — she's nothing to do with solicitors, as far as I know.'

'Which is much to her credit. No, don't worry, sergeant; she can appear in the time-honoured, and quite legitimate, role of Prisoner's Friend. Send a car for her.'

Purbright's surmise that Miss Teatime might have a little friendship left over for the Prosecutor as well proved correct. He had completed all but one of his planned interviews at the Floradora Club, when he was told that Miss Teatime had come out from town and would like a word with him.

The inspector was occupying the same office, but he had moved from the late proprietor's desk, the pretentious acreage of which he disliked, to a smaller one on the other side of the room.

Miss Teatime entered in as eager and genial a manner as if she were the sole beneficiary arriving for the reading of a will.

'I do hope,' she said, sitting in the chair that Purbright had fetched for her, 'that I have done nothing improper in respect of public funds by soliciting another lift in one of your nice police cars. They are most comfortable and they smell of pine forests.'

Purbright said he was glad that it had been possible to oblige her in so small a matter. He trusted she had found her friend Mr Tudor well and that she had been able to give him such advice as he required.

Miss Teatime's mouth retained her smile, but at the corner appeared a little twist of astuteness, of good-natured reproof.

'Come, inspector, you must have seen enough of Mr Tudor by now to realise that he is a very odious gentleman indeed, and a vicious.'

'You conveyed a somewhat different impression the other day,' Purbright said drily.

'That was before he saw fit to presume upon mutual acquaintance in order to try and involve me in his squalid activities. If there is one thing I learned from my mother's side of the family (all those dreadful marquesses) it is to abhor presumption on acquaintance.'

The inspector inclined his head in agreement. 'I must admit I was surprised when he asked to see you, Miss Teatime. You must have been most embarrassed.'

'It was his request that was embarrassing, Mr Purbright. He wishes me to intercede on his behalf, in order — as I think he expressed it — to prevent your "pinning a rap on him". Have I got that right? Pinning a rap? It sounds like some sort of makeshift costume, but I think I am worldly enough to know that he was probably referring to an impending criminal charge.'

'A murder charge, in point of fact.'

Miss Teatime shook her head. 'I feared as much.'

After a short silence, she said: 'To be quite candid, Mr Purbright, and with the greatest reluctance, I have to record my conviction that Mr Tudor has not killed anybody for some little while.'

'Why, do you suppose, should the man be so reluctant to explain his presence in Flaxborough if what you believe is true?'

She smiled. 'You may perhaps have noticed, inspector, that the bigger a scoundrel a man is, the more zealously he proclaims some mystical or high-sounding abstraction or other.'

The inspector considered. 'Patriotism? Confidentiality? Biological detergents? That sort of thing?'

'Precisely. The catchword of which Mr Tudor is especially enamoured is Honour. That is the concept, I understand, that is traditionally employed to dignify the goings-on of Mediterranean assassins, womanisers, and generals who like locking people up. In his particular case, I fancy the word connotes secretiveness.'

'Do you know why he's here?'

'I believe I do, inspector.'

'And are you going to tell me?'

Miss Teatime opened her reticule and took out cheroots and matches. 'For what it is worth,' she said.

Purbright looked about the desk top for an ashtray. There was none in sight. He pulled open the shallow drawer before him.

'You will be unable,' said Miss Teatime, 'to obtain any confirmation from Mr Tudor, but my belief is that he came to Flaxborough not to commit a crime but to prevent one of his minor associates from doing so.'

Purbright ceased rummaging in the drawer. He looked at her with suddenly sharpened attention.

'He spoke of family troubles, you see,' Miss Teatime explained. 'My understanding is that "family" is a term used very broadly in Mr Tudor's sense. It probably embraces all those co-religionists of similar occupation but not necessarily of like eminence.'

'Fellow olive oil importers?' suggested the inspector.

Miss Teatime smiled. 'We are a little behind the times, inspector — or, rather, Mr Tudor imagines we are. The current pretension in his circle is to banking interests and something they call real estate.'

She lit her small cigar, blew out the match and sat holding it like an exhibit. Purbright renewed his search of the drawer and came across a small tin box. He took off the lid. The box contained a number of tiny, semi-transparent rectangles. He tipped these out upon a sheet of paper and set the empty tin before Miss Teatime.

'Did Tudor know the identity of this associate you think he wished to restrain?'

'I am sure he did not. But he was confident that if such a person had arrived here, he would recognise him.'

Purbright ruminatively shifted the little rectangles about with the point of a pencil. They had rounded corners and one face of each was shinier than its reverse.

'You didn't happen to know Mr Hatch, I suppose,' he said.

'Only as a regular contributor to one or another of our charities. It would not be kind to draw from that the inference that he had a troubled conscience, of course.'

'Certainly not,' Purbright agreed. He thought he had never heard a charge of turpitude more delicately framed.

There was a folder by his elbow. He opened it and sorted through papers until he found the letter that Hatch had received, the letter threatening his life.

'Do you think,' he asked Miss Teatime, 'that Tudor knew Hatch to be the man whose murder was intended?'

She considered.

Purbright spoke again before she could reply. 'Or was his attendance at the banquet here last night purely fortuitous? I ask you that because I recall that you provided him with the ticket.'

She nodded. 'True. I have been wondering ever since if he had precise knowledge of what was going to happen. I am inclined to doubt it.'

'Might he not, in fact, have been less concerned to stop a murder than to take over for himself the protection — as he would understand the word — of a profitable sub-legal enterprise?'

The inspector saw the slightly pained expression on Miss Teatime's face and added hastily: 'The argument is purely hypothetical, naturally.'

She brightened at once. 'I always try to adopt a balanced view, Mr Purbright. Especially when there exists a personal commitment of the kind, for instance, that a ticket agency implies. However, I do not quarrel with your assessment of Mr Tudor's capabilities. Hypothetically speaking, if he were to pass wind it would rain granite chips.'

When Miss Teatime had gone, a young uniformed constable who was acting as doorman and messenger was sent by the inspector to fetch coffee. Purbright felt a trifle mean at having delayed the order. The Floradora coffee was so odd though (it conformed to a prescription of Mrs Hatch's own devising and contained the salt and soda that she warmly declared made 'all the difference', as, indeed they did) that he had lacked courage to ask Miss Teatime to share it. In any case, there was no whisky available, the club's entire stock having been distributed by the raiding party from Brocklestone.

The young constable tip-toed with great care and respect across the office and set the cup down by Purbright's arm. The inspector murmured his thanks and continued to read a transcript of his earlier tape-recorded interview with a member of the Mackintosh-Brooke team — the one who had discovered in the books some astonishing figures relating to meat extract.

Suddenly Purbright heard the young constable gasp 'Oh, sir!'

He looked up.

The constable was staring at the anonymous letter that Hatch had received from America. No, not at the letter, Purbright realised; at the envelope. The constable's face registered surprise, delight and trepidation, all at once.

'Oh, sir!' he said again. Purbright recognised the kind of voice in which schoolboys acknowledge the autographs of footballers.

'Well?' Purbright prompted, trying to recall the constable's name. Candle? Cornell?

'It's a first day cover, sir,' declared the young constable, husky with awe. 'Excuse me, sir, but do you think I . . do you think it would be . . .'

'Hold on a minute.' Cordwell — that was it. 'Hadn't you better tell me, Mr Cordwell, just what you have seen that is so exciting?'

Cordwell swallowed, blushed, and swallowed again. He leaned closer and pointed to the envelope, then at the stamp and the postmark.

'First day cover, sir,' he repeated. 'That means it was posted on the first day of a new issue. The postmark — there, you see, sir — is June the Eighth. And that is when this stamp was first on sale. Sir, if it would be possible — I mean when this envelope isn't needed any more . . .'

'May I,' the inspector interrupted, 'ask how you come to know these fascinating things?'

'Well, philately happens to be my hobby, sir. I've been collecting stamps for quite a while.'

'I see.' Purbright unclipped the envelope from its letter. 'And is there anything particularly notable about this stamp, apart from the date of cancellation?'

'Oh, yes, sir. This is the very first American issue showing a president during his lifetime. I'm not sure, but I believe Mr Nixon had the rules changed himself. Anyway, it's a very collectable item.'

Purbright smiled. 'In other words, you want me to purloin this for you when it's not wanted any more as evidence.'

Another blush spread upwards from Constable Cordwell's collar. 'That would be really very good of you, sir.' He added after a pause. 'My wife would be a lot happier, too.'

Purbright had a fleet vision of the Cordwells' connubial couch, littered with Cape of Good Hope Triangulars during a joint session with the stamp album. 'Don't tell me *she*'s a philatelist?'

'Oh, no, sir. But she forgot to post the letter containing our self-addressed envelopes that I was supposed to be sending a dealer in New York for him to get stamped for us and put in the mail. I'm afraid I was a bit cross with her.'

'That is a usual arrangement is it — for stamp firms to post letters for clients on particular days?'

'Quite usual, sir.'

For a while, Purbright was silent. As he pondered, his eye strayed to the heap of flimsy little rectangles. A few had been blown across the desk by the movement of air occasioned by Cordwell's arrival.

The constable noticed them too.

'They're called hinges, aren't they?' Purbright said to him.

'That's right, sir. Or mounts. For mounting stamps on the page.' Cordwell gave the explanation with a trace of puzzlement in his voice. A deep one, this bloke Purbright.

'Sit down, Mr Cordwell.' Purbright indicated the chair vacated by Miss Teatime. 'I want you to look at something and tell me if it means anything to you.' He took from his folder the copy of the cablegram that had been brought him by Miss Ryland.

Sitting very straight, and with the paper held before him like a hymn book, the constable slowly and conscientiously read the message through. And once again, the inspector observed, Cordwell was being stirred by some strange inner enthusiasm.

'Good lord!' Cordwell exclaimed at last, adding 'sir' as a merely reflexive concession. He looked with shining eye at Purbright. 'They're fearfully rare, you know.'

'Indeed?'

'Not half, sir. They reckon there are only five in existence — apart from the one at the Vatican, and *that* isn't likely to get into circulation, is it, sir?'

'I wouldn't know,' said Purbright, momentarily depressed by Cordwell's esoteric zeal. He recovered. 'Look, I want you to treat me as an untutored child for a while and explain in simple terms what this is all about. Don't be nervous, but I believe you have the key to something extremely important.'

The constable regarded him earnestly, cleared his throat and took breath.

'Well, sir,' he began, 'as you'll have gathered, it's about stamps.'

Chapter Twenty

Purbright passed on to the chief constable an edited version of Cordwell's lecture, and was pleasantly surprised by Mr Chubb's familiarity with terms that might otherwise have made the interview hard going. Oh, yes, Mr Chubb assured him, he knew what a transposed vignette was; he once had spotted one himself. It was in a packet of approvals that had come his way when he was at school, and he had sold it to another boy for five shillings. He didn't dare think what such a stamp would be worth today.

'Enough to make it a readily negotiable piece of property, apparently,' said Purbright, 'to say nothing of a convenient international investment for anyone who wishes to salt away some questionably acquired cash.'

Mr Chubb took his point, but thought it a great shame that even so wholesome and instructive a schoolboys' hobby as stamp-collecting should be made to serve the ends of criminals.

Into which mood of reflection upon human perversity, Purbright chose to toss a startling announcement.

'I was speaking over the transatlantic telephone at four o'clock this afternoon to a Captain Michael West, of the New York police.'

Mr Chubb at first looked politely querulous, as if he were not quite sure where New York was. Then he peered at Purbright with sharper attention, almost alarm.

'New York, *America?*'

'That New York, yes, sir.'

'I trust you had some very good reason, Mr Purbright. Authorisation for things like that is terribly difficult to obtain, even in advance. Retrospectively . . . good heavens!'

Purbright thought he had not seen the chief constable look so concerned since the last hard-pad outbreak.

'It was not a very lengthy call, sir. There seemed no better way to get quick and accurate answers to certain vital questions. And West is a most charming and intelligent man. He once visited Flaxborough.'

This mitigating circumstance earned a pleasant 'Oh, really?' from Mr Chubb.

'The Interpol people put me on to him,' the inspector explained. 'It was to his station — precinct house, I think is the New York term — that the letter purporting to prophesy our murder was sent. He had kept the letter itself on file, of course, but it was mainly the envelope I wanted to talk about. Fortunately, it hadn't been thrown away. He was able to turn both up straight away.'

Purbright placed before Mr Chubb the envelope that had so intrigued constable Cordwell.

'Captain West and I made what might be called a comparison by description. We found enough points of similarity to suggest very strongly indeed that both envelopes — and both letters — had a common authorship, certainly a common source.

'The dimensions of the envelopes checked exactly. Postmarks were identical. Same district, same time. The ink and style of addressing were more difficult to compare in the circumstances, but we could spot no obvious discrepancy. The stamps were of different denominations, but they belonged to the same new commemorative issue.

'Now, sir; perhaps we can consider the letters. The first is a warning to the police — the American police, who reasonably might be expected to pass the warning on — that a Mafia-style murder is planned to take place in

Flaxborough. No names are offered, only the location.

'The second letter is very different. It is a threat to a specific person, and it is addressed to that person direct. Subsequently, the man who gets the letter, and, again as one might expect, reports it to us, is found murdered.

'As I say, sir, the letters seem utterly different in intention. One, an informer's tip-off; the other, a death sentence. Each, though, has a ring of authenticity. And because they turn up at different times in the hands of unrelated and widely separated people, each seems to reinforce the credibility of the other.

'But only so long' — Purbright spoke more slowly and deliberately — 'as the letters remain three thousand miles apart and are not examined jointly for signs of their having been concocted by the same writer. And why, after all, should they not so remain?'

The chief constable hoped very much that the question was rhetorical, because he could not have answered it to save his life. He suspected that Purbright, in some subtle way, was getting his own back for the rebuke over the telephone call.

'Why, indeed,' murmured Mr Chubb, forcing a smile.

'You will, of course, have raced ahead and deduced the conclusions that Captain West and I reached,' said Purbright, 'but I shall outline them nonetheless, if you don't object, sir.'

Mr Chubb magnanimously waved him on.

'We agreed at once that the two letters constituted a cleverly trailed red herring, the object of which was persuasively to lay advance blame for an intended murder upon some actual but amorphous criminal organisation. The would-be murderer, we decided, was almost certain to be someone in this country, not in America — someone who knew enough about his victim's business activities to realise that they rendered him liable to extortion.

'But how had the letters come to be mailed in a city on the other side of the Atlantic? Captain West inclined to the idea of an accomplice, but wasn't happy about the peculiar way in which the letter to the American police had been addressed. Wouldn't a collaborator in New York have taken the trouble to specify at least the street and district?'

'Good point,' said the chief constable, who had been trying to think if this West could have been the rather likeable American he had chatted to a dozen or more years ago during some official visit or other. An unveiling, was it? Nice chap. Rose grower.

A knock at the door presaged the entry of Sergeant Love. He was accompanied by a small, wiry man, with a large bald head. The head was sun-tanned to the colour of pumpkin rind and very shiny. It was like some cherished and regularly rubbed-up domestic utensil.

'Here's Doctor Fergusson, sir,' the sergeant announced.

Some brisk hand-shaking ensued. The police surgeon was an energetic mover who seemed perpetually to be desirous of embarking upon a journey.

'I asked Doctor Fergusson along to make an official examination,' Purbright explained to Mr Chubb. He turned to Love. 'All right, sergeant, you may fetch Mr Amis now. I think he's in the lounge next to that roulette wheel place.'

'Ay-ay-ay-ay . . .' This sound of Scottish restlessness came from Dr Fergusson, who had stepped to the window and was staring out, as upon a train timetable in the sky.

Two minutes went by.

Mr Chubb leaned close to Purbright and spoke very softly. 'Examination? I'm afraid I don't quite follow.' He kept his eyes on Fergusson's back, where the doctor's hands were engaged in a small, impatient wrestling match.

The inspector's reply was just as quietly delivered. 'Sorry, sir; I should have explained. The odds are that . . .'

Dr Fergusson wheeled round suddenly from the window. He was glaring at his watch. 'Look here,' he said, 'I don't want to mess up your routine or anything, but I do happen to have left something pretty urgent to do in town. Could you let me have half an hour?' He was already at the door, pulling it open. 'No, twenty minutes. I'll be back in twenty minutes. All right?'

The last two words reached them faintly through the closing door. Mr Chubb looked much displeased and said he really thought Fergusson was the limit. What had he come for, anyway? Purbright told him. He added his opinion that half an hour's delay would make no material difference.

Another minute elapsed without further sign of Love or his charge.

Purbright did some re-arranging of things on the desk top. He smiled reflectively. 'We were rather lucky, you know, sir,' he said, 'in turning up such extraordinarily quick workers as those New York people. I put our question of whether there was a firm of stamp dealers in their locality whose name began with the letters O, X and O, and in less than two hours they rang back having not only traced the firm but most perceptively interviewed one of its principals.'

When Edmund Amis arrived, he entered the office in advance of Love and without knocking. He was wearing a lightweight tweed suit, the cut and quality of which the chief constable immediately noticed and approved. His manner was confident, his air of recognition friendly. With a very white handkerchief, he touched his mouth and chin. 'I hope I haven't kept you, gentlemen; I was taking some tea.' The mouth was — Purbright discovered the word tuck-shop in his mind and worked from that — chubby. A chubby mouth, boy-like. Yet the flesh round and under the jaw was as flaccid as a middle-aged matron's.

Purbright introduced the chief constable. Amis nodded, accepted a chair and pulled up enough neatly creased trouser leg to reveal socks in pale blue silk crochet. He glanced with polite interest at Love's manipulation of buttons on a tape recorder.

'Let us,' said Purbright, 'come straight to the point, Mr Amis — or to *a* point, rather. Some rather odd features have come to light in the records of this club's finances. I must ask you first of all if you have any knowledge of them.'

'If you mean by "odd" dishonest, the answer is no.'

'Oh, I do not wish to strain the word at this stage beyond its meaning of unusual, unexpected — interesting, if you like.'

'I think you are going to have to give me a specific example, inspector.'

'Very well.' Purbright referred to a set of figures in the file before him. 'On 18 February this year, a cheque was issued in favour of Oxo — presumably the beef extract manufacturers.' He looked up. 'Correct?'

'If what you have there is a record of the cheque counterfoils, that is your answer, I suppose. I can scarcely be expected to recall from memory one single cheque out of all that go to our suppliers.'

'The amount,' said Purbright, 'is £775. That would buy rather a lot of beef cubes, wouldn't it, sir?'

After a brief ensuing silence, the small explosion of laughter from Amis sounded spontaneous and curiously guileless. Mr Chubb, who had retired to stand in the background, stared at him and wondered.

'It would, indeed,' said Amis, most amiably 'We shall have to see what is on the invoice. Someone's slipped up, obviously.'

The inspector referred again to his list. 'It would appear that the club was out of beef cubes again by 30 May. The supply that was ordered on that occasion cost £1120.'

Amis did not laugh a second time. He ran a finger slowly along his plump jaw-line and stared thoughtfully into the middle distance. He turned to Purbright and indicated his folio. 'Have a look at the invoice. As you say, there *is* something odd about this.'

The inspector gazed back, levelly. 'No invoice has been found, Mr Amis. And no receipt. Indeed, during the past fourteen months a total of nearly £4000 is indicated by these "Oxo" counterfoils, yet not one invoice or receipt appears to exist.'

Amis pondered. The others watched him. He undeniably was taking his time, yet seemed somehow not to be playing for time. At last, he shrugged. 'I'm sorry, inspector, but I really can't imagine what he'd been doing.'

'He?' echoed Purbright at once. 'Whom do you mean by "he"?'

Amis's eyes widened. 'Poor old Hatch. Who else?' He leaned forward. 'Now, look, inspector, Hatch liked to refer to me as his private secretary. In fact, I was his hired help, that's all. One thing I certainly was not, and that was the company secretary.'

'But you did handle cheques.'

'As an office boy might be said to handle cheques. Hatch expected all his employees to muck in, as he rather disgustingly put it.'

'It was not uncommon, I understand, sir, for you to take a batch of cheques for signature before all the details had been filled in, and for you then to complete them in your own time. Am I right?'

'That did happen occasionally. Mr Hatch's movements were pretty unpredictable. One had to catch him when one could.'

Hatch, catch, batch flitted ridiculously through Purbright's brain. He said: 'From this point, Mr Amis, I am going to have to ask you questions of a more searching nature. It is your right to have advice as to how to answer them — if, indeed, you wish to answer them at all. Do you want your solicitor to be present?'

Amis was silent a moment. Then a faint, pouting smile, a smirk of mock contrition. 'Oh, dear,' he said, very quietly; and again, 'Oh, dear.'

Purbright waited.

Amis sniffed, suddenly resolute. 'No, I think we can dispense with solicitors. The man who would really have had need of one is out of the picture now. But I've a fair idea what sort of thing you've dug up. And you possibly think I should have guessed earlier, and done something about it. That's your drift, isn't it?'

There was in the easy posture, the good-naturedly chiding tone of the man, that essence of assured superiority which the unwary so often mistake for friendliness.

'Not at all,' Purbright replied. 'You are in no danger of being charged with collusion, Mr Amis.'

'Well, thank goodness for that. I mean, I shouldn't be altogether flabbergasted if you were to tell me that there had been tax fiddles here, or even something a bit close to the wind where the play and the girls are concerned. You follow? I mean to say, that sort of malarky does go on in clubs. But don't worry, Hatch was too sharp to give me any hints, let alone make me a partner in crime. Do you know why he gave me this job, inspector? Simply because he thought it would be rather posh to have a private secretary. So he installed one. Just as he put that ridiculous swimming pool in his garden. I feel I have a sort of kinship with that pool. We're both status symbols.'

'Do you feel kinship with his Olson and Morgan?' Purbright asked.

'I beg your pardon?'

There had been a pause, certainly, before Amis's response, but Purbright was not sure whether it betokened guilt or puzzlement. Probably, he told himself, the latter. The man's undiminished pleasantness of manner implied anxiety to understand a witticism that had not quite connected.

'I was referring to Mr Hatch's somewhat expensive sporting gun,' Purbright explained.

Chapter Twenty-one

'Ah.' Amis smiled. 'Yes, it would be an expensive one, naturally.'

'You are not a shooting man, yourself, sir?'

'I'm afraid not. You will not find me responding satisfactorily to the dropping of famous names in that department, inspector.'

'A more peaceable occupation, perhaps, would appeal to you?'

'Conceivably.'

'Let us see, then, if I may drop a name to which you *will* respond. One with essentially pacific associations.'

Purbright considered, or pretended to. The three others in the room watched him: Mr Chubb gravely, Sergeant Love with one eye on his tape, Amis in patience.

'Gibbons,' said the inspector.

'*The Decline and Fall* gentleman,' said Amis at once. '*Of the Roman Empire*.' Love's expression warmed to admiration: he was an avid spectator of television quiz games. But Purbright shook his head.

'That one, I think you'll find, was Gibbon singular. Gibbons is the name on a famous and exhaustive catalogue of postage stamps.'

In his corner, Mr Chubb nodded in concurrence.

'We'll try another,' Purbright said. 'How do you react to the resonance of the Oxonia Philatelic Trading Corporation? Of New York and London?'

A small but noticeable change had affected Amis's amiability. It now was edged with brittleness.

'So unlikely a title must be genuine. I presume we have arrived at the heavy hinting stage, have we, inspector?'

'No, sir. At the honest explanation stage, I should have hoped. Tell me this for a start. When you handed Hatch an uncompleted cheque made out to Oxo for him to sign in that off-handed and very unbusinesslike way that he probably imagined was appropriate to being rich, was it not with the clear intention of expanding "Oxo" to Oxonia, adding the rest of the firm's title and finally inserting the amount — a substantial amount — for payment?'

Amis regarded him with a sort of repressed derision — rather like indigestion, except that laughter rather than wind was trying to come up.

The inspector did not wait long before pursuing his theme.

'And did you not pay to the London branch of Oxonia by the method I have described a total of' — he bent forward to consult a slip of paper — 'of just under £4000 since February of last year?'

Spectator Love hurriedly looked away, but his eyes were already bulging and his lips funnelled.

'For what?' asked Amis, as quietly as he could, it seemed, lest his amusement erupt.

'For a number of rare stamps you had commissioned the firm to obtain for you, notably a set of five misprints from the two-and-a-half lire Vatican City issue of 1932.'

Amis turned up his eyes. 'Dear god,' he sighed, 'do I look like a stamp collector?'

Purbright deputised with an answer. 'Possibly not, sir; but one does not have to look like an engraver in order to draw notes from a bank. A valuable stamp is as good as a load of currency: better, because it is less likely to depreciate and it can be more privately negotiated.'

'Two and a half lire doesn't sound much like a load of currency, not even by 1932 standards.'

Purbright sighed. 'You really must stop trying to sell your intelligence short, Mr Amis. This is your desk, is it not?'

'Until you arrived, yes.' The humorous attitude was back, but it was wry now, and had sharper calculation behind it.

The inspector opened the drawer. He picked out a pinch of stamp hinges and let them flutter to the desk surface in front of Amis. There was a lens in the drawer and close by, a pair of tweezers and a rectangular piece of plastic, rather like a rule, except that its edges were serrated.

'You may claim not to look like a stamp collector, but you seem to have acquired some of the tools of the trade.' Purbright picked up the toothed rule. 'Even a perforation gauge. Remember the specifications of the Naked Nuns, Mr Amis? Nineteen and fifteen?'

A grin. 'Bit young for nuns, surely?'

'Exactly what *we* thought when we first heard of them.' Purbright, too, was smiling. ' "Perf. nineteen, fifteen . . ." Rather like one of the odder brothel advertisements, with "perf" for perfect — the standard exaggeration, of course.' He heard from the outfield Mr Chubb's little cough of rebuke. 'Now we know better. Nineteen perforations on the horizontal sides, fifteen on the vertical. And "Naked Nun" the trade nickname for the result of the rather puckish philatelic mishap in 1932 whereby two vignette plates were transposed at the printers.'

Purbright, happening to glance at Love, saw on his face so plain a plea for curiosity to be satisfied at once that he amplified the account for the sergeant's special benefit.

'The frame of the stamp depicted a procession of nuns, and the oval insertion, the so-called head plate, should have been a portrait of Pope Pius the Eleventh. But what actually appeared was one of Manet's "Olympia." '

'Olympia?' echoed Love, unable to help himself.

'A famous nude painting, sergeant.'

'French,' added Amis, drawing upon an almost depleted reserve of waggish confidence. Purbright he addressed with more seriousness.

'It is obvious that I should have known better than to pretend absolute ignorance, inspector. I simply didn't want to be drawn into an investigation of Hatch's affairs. I might add that the possibility of my receiving attention from his gangster friends didn't much appeal either.'

'Ah, yes, his Mafia associations. What do you know about those, Mr Amis?'

'Virtually nothing. Except that Hatch was having to pay out money. Protection money, I suppose one would call it. Club proprietors do tend to get involved with that sort of thing. It's true, of course, that I know a little about stamps. I advised Hatch on which ones he should buy. It is possible that he used some of them to meet his protection bills. I don't know. As you say, though, stamps are negotiable.'

Purbright nodded. 'I'm so glad you've been frank, sir. This stamps business had been puzzling us a good deal. Hatch was a man of some accomplishment, but I couldn't quite see him as an informed enthusiast in so specialised a field.'

Both men looked amused at the thought. Amis was still smiling when the inspector said casually:

'I suppose, then, that it was you and not Hatch who mailed that packet of letters to New York for Oxonia to give them first-day post under the new presidential commemorative issue.'

At the end of some seconds' silence, Amis said merely: 'First I've heard of it.' He did not sound as if he expected to be believed.

'I have to admire the quickness of thinking it displayed,' Purbright said. 'The descent upon the club of the gentlemen from Mackintosh-Brooke must have left you very little time to prepare for the somewhat drastic measure that their inquisitiveness was going to force you to take. From an ordinary audit, you had nothing to fear. The books showed no payments that hadn't received Hatch's authority or were outside the normal scope of his business. But an efficiency investigation — that was something different. It was bound to bring into question a catering system that required as big an outlay on beef cubes as on whisky.'

Amis, half rising from his chair, began to say something. Purbright gestured him to silence. As Amis hung in an immobile crouch between sitting and standing, the inspector began to recite, quite softly as if it were designed to give comfort, the formal warning that he was soon to be charged with murder.

Before he had quite finished, the door was opened brusquely and Fergusson was back: spry, bustling, between trains.

'Right, then,' Fergusson said, immediately the caution had been delivered. He glanced rapidly from one to another of those in the room, as if they were contestants in a race who had been waiting for him to return with the starting pistol.

Purbright frowned at him. 'Just a moment, doctor, if you don't mind.' He turned again to Amis. 'Do you wish to say anything at this stage?'

'Is it . . .' Amis, whose fingers had been straying restlessly about the flesh of neck and jaw, had discovered a long whisker in isolation just below his left ear and was pulling it so that the skin there rose in a little peak — 'Is that usual?' He was sitting again, but slumped forward slightly. To look at Purbright, while not relinquishing the whisker, he had to twist his head upward and sideways. It gave him a curiously submissive, almost cringing air. *Is that usual?* The naïvéte of the question, the unhappy deference it implied, released in Purbright a sudden loathing for what was going on.

'You must decide for yourself, Mr Amis,' he said, flatly. 'The charge will be made formally at the police station, to which you will be taken now. You may confer with your solicitor as soon as you wish. Every facility will be given you.'

Amis departed, without another word, in the cheerful custody of Sergeant Love. He was listless, grey-faced, flabby. He did not look at all like a private secretary. He did not look like a murderer, either. His errant single hair was still bothering him, and his preoccupation with it made him stumble at the door.

'And *now* what, for Christ's sake?' demanded Doctor Fergusson of the inspector and Mr Chubb in an indignant sweep from one to the other. His voice had a bagpipe-ish squeak.'

Purbright apologised and explained.

'I didn't expect him to cave in. In a sense, I didn't want him to. It somehow makes the affair that much more squalid. If he hadn't, of course, he would have been asked to submit to a simple medical examination. There's almost certainly a deep bruise on his right shoulder. It should still be obvious at remand reception, though.'

Fergusson was mollified by the mention of a bruise. 'Ah. The gun. Aye.' He paused. 'Aye, but if everybody who fired a shot gun got bruised by the recoil, half my patients would be out of commission by the end of the first week of the pheasant season. It's long odds, Purbright.'

'Not all that long. Amis is a townsman, a Londoner. And not in the tweedy week-ending set, either. A twelve-bore would kick him like a cannon.'

'That's perfectly true, doctor,' the chief constable confirmed, in order to get into a conversation from which he suspected Fergusson aimed to extract credit. 'It is also true, as Mr Purbright observed to me earlier, that the man stank of liniment. A shrewd point, I thought.'
Mr Chubb smirked frostily. 'But one that might escape the notice of someone always using the stuff in the course of his trade, perhaps?'

'Ah, detection! Detection!'

With which sardonic cry, the doctor abruptly departed.

For perhaps a minute, Mr Chubb stood in silent and motionless effort to conquer the outrageous impression that Fergusson had slapped him on the back. But he did not prevail.

Purbright spoke to him.

'I must get over to Fen Street now, sir. Do you wish to come?'

'I think not, Mr Purbright. Unless there is something that cannot wait until morning.'

'No, sir.'

'What about a warrant, by the way? You'll be searching the fellow's flat, I take it.'

'Tomorrow.'

'For the stamps?'

Purbright shrugged. 'He may tell us where they are. If not, I doubt if we shall ever find them. Five small scraps of paper.'

The chief constable looked concerned.

'Oh, the case doesn't depend on them, sir,' Purbright said. 'Oxonia's London manager told me over the phone that Hatch collected his buys in person and always had the cheque ready. The manager says he can identify Hatch whenever we want him to. He described him to me just to prove it.'

'Amis, I suppose.'

'Yes, sir.'

'I wonder,' said Mr Chubb a little later, 'how the man consistently kept his employer ignorant of these dealings. There must have been letters sometimes, and they would have been addressed to Hatch.'

'At his club, sir. Where Amis was a conscientious early starter, whose job it was to open the mail, anyway. Telegrams might have been more tricky; my guess is that he told Oxonia to curb their agents' exuberance after he'd received that wire from Philadelphia that gave our Miss Ryland nightmares about white slaving.'

Purbright gathered his papers and put them in a case. This and the tape recorder he carried to the door. He looked, the chief constable regretfully reflected, rather more like a traveller checking out of an hotel room than an inspector of police.

The constable on duty in the corridor jerked out of some gloomy reverie and saluted. Purbright made a face at him and told him to go and get himself a meal.

On their way to the car park, the chief constable stopped and looked back. Purbright turned, too. Among the windows of the single-storey building they had just left, there had been nailed a square of hardboard, like an eye-patch.

'You haven't told me, you know,' said Mr Chubb, 'why you were so confident that an outsider couldn't have shot that poor fellow. The gangster person, for instance. Or even Crispin — yes, I know he's a councillor, but he gets up to some pretty queer tricks, they tell me.'

Purbright pointed. 'Hatch's gun was kept in that room, the one next to the office. It would have to be brought out and hidden — behind the pile of planks there, for instance — before too many customers were milling around the club. I can't see how either Tudor or Crispin could have done that. And whoever subsequently rammed the gun barrel through the window and pulled the trigger must have known for an absolute certainty who was inside that washroom. It must have been someone who had been with Hatch up to that moment, and actually seen him go in to have a wash.'

'That does seem very logical, Mr Purbright,' agreed the chief constable, 'but what was to prevent a person lurking in the grounds — a scoundrel such as what's-his-name, Tudor — from taking a shot at his victim, his "contract" — was that the word? — as soon as poor Hatch came in and put the light on?'

'Frosted glass, sir,' said Purbright.

They resumed their way to their separate cars. Mr Chubb drove away in his at once. The inspector's took some time to start. It usually did.

MORE
GREAT READING
FROM
Robert B. Parker
"Robert B. Parker
has taken his place
beside Dashiell Hammett,
Raymond Chandler, and Ross
MacDonald."—The Boston Globe
Looking for
Rachel Wallace $2.50 15316-6
Early Autumn $2.50 12214-7
A Savage Place $2.95 18095-3
Also, look for these upcoming Parker mysteries in 1983:
Ceremony ....April
The Godwulf Manuscript ....May
God Save the Child ....June
Mortal Stakes ....July
Promised Land ....August
The Judas Goat ....September
At your local bookstore or use this handy coupon for ordering:
Dell
DELL BOOKS
P.O. BOX 1000, PINE BROOK, N.J. 07058-1000
Please send me the books I have checked above. I am enclosing $ ________ (please add 75c per copy to cover postage and handling). Send check or money order—no cash or C.O.D.'s. Please allow up to 8 weeks for shipment.
Mr./Mrs./Miss ________
Address ________
City ________ State/Zip ________